LETHAL

OPERATION JUSTICE FORCE BOOK ONE

REESE KNIGHTLEY

Lethal (Operation Justice Force Book One)
Copyright © 2022 Reese Knightley
ALL RIGHTS RESERVED

Warnings
Please be advised that this book is intended for adult readers age eighteen and older due to sexually explicit content, language, and violence.

This is a work of fiction. Names, characters, places, and incidents either are the product of the author's imagination or are used fictitiously, and any resemblance to the actual person, living or dead, business establishments, events, or locales is entirely coincidental. This is a work of fiction and should be treated as such.

All rights reserved.
No part of this book may be reproduced in any form or by any electronic or mechanical means, including information storage and retrieval systems, without the written permission from the author, except for the use of brief quotations in a book review.

Cover image (c) 2021 Wander Aguiar Photography LLC https://www.wanderbookclub.com/

Cover model SOJ

Disclaimer—Cover content is for illustrative purposes only. Any person depicted on the cover is a model.

Cover Art: Reese Dante reesedante.com

Editing provided by Heidi Ryan of Amour the Line Editing
www.facebook.com/amourthelineediting

Interior Design and Formatting provided by
Stacey Blake of Champagne Book Design –
www.champagnebookdesign.com

Copyright and Trademark Acknowledgments: All products/brand names/Trademarks mentioned are registered trademarks of their respective holders/companies.

Please note—There is a large cast of characters in this book. The Pegasus roster can be located at the back of the book.

LETHAL

CHAPTER ONE

Adam

"SON OF A BITCH."

Yeah, getting shot was not a good way to start the day, but it could have been worse.

Adam pressed the edge of his t-shirt against the bullet wound in his left side and slipped down the alley, hugging the shadows. When running footsteps drew near, he stepped back against the damp brick wall.

With the Ruger—fully loaded and silenced—clenched in his grip, he pushed hard into his side to stem the flow of blood.

He needed to reassess his attacker's desire to kill him.

The footsteps stopped inside the alley and Adam went completely still, a trained act not many could accomplish, but one he'd learned while young, stay still or be found. As he grew older, it became stay still or be killed.

The darkly dressed figure of a man stepped into the dark, stained alley, staying in the shadows, hovering on the fringes and slipping in unnoticed, much like Adam had done. Well, it was exactly like he'd done.

He was pretty sure they'd send one of their best to kill him, but this guy was about to have a really bad day. When someone missed their first shot at him, they rarely, if ever, got another.

He didn't even lift his arm all the way. Bending his elbow, he shot from waist high and hit the concrete next to the man's head. The wall cracked, the blowback was immediate, and the crash of trash cans and cursing were his cue. He would have tried for a leg shot, but with the darkness and his loss of blood, shooting the wall was the best he could do.

If the guy kept coming, Adam would shoot to kill. Anything less was asking to get dead.

Clenching his teeth, he silently lunged across the alley and grabbed the ladder, climbing the fire escape until he reached the roof. He ran toward the access door.

Halfway across the roof, bullets peppered the tar-covered slabs behind him.

Damned bastard! When the tables were turned, and trust him, the tables would be turned, whoever this guy was, was in for a world of hurt.

"You can run, Sphinx, but you can't hide!"

He stumbled and righted himself, then lunged for the entrance of the apartment building.

That fucking voice rang in his head, blowing his mind.

When he reached the door, he ducked inside and slammed back against the wall.

He knew that voice! Fucking hell. He sucked in several savage breaths.

Using the doorjamb for cover, he fired back out the door, his aim high. This time, he meant to miss.

"Keep chasing me and you won't live to see another birthday," he hollered back and then held his breath, waiting for that deep, rasping tone.

"I'll see you in hell first." The man's shout accompanied a hail of bullets that pinged the doorway near Adam's head.

He scowled. He wasn't mistaken about that voice.

When the edge of the doorway splintered apart, he swung his face away to avoid flying wood and debris. Swinging his arm around, he fired two more shots before leaping down the stairs. Releasing his hold against his dripping wound, he slammed a new clip into the chamber.

Two floors down, he shoved open the rickety interior door and ran down the stained carpeted hallway until he reached a closed apartment door.

With a silent apology to the occupants, he kicked in the door, ran across the living room, and left by way of their balcony. Adrenaline kicked in and he flew over the side, snagging the metal railing to stop his fall. He hung suspended by one hand. His side burned and the blood made the material of his pants wet and sticky. Fucking hell, these were his best pair of pants.

"But you're alive," he muttered, thinking about the man who was after him. Yeah, he was damned lucky.

Beneath him lay the dark parking lot. Its wet surface ran along the back of the building, but he knew it was too far of a drop to the pavement or the cars below. Risking a broken limb wasn't in the cards. A commercial trash can was underneath the balcony to the left with the metal top closed. Landing in the trash wasn't an option.

Swinging his body, he dropped down to the balcony

below. Nearer to the top of the cars now, he gauged the distance. Closer, but not by much.

Snick, snick.

Bullets hit the stucco near his head, and he raced to the far side of the flowerpot-filled patio and climbed over the railing.

A bullet bounced off the metal near his hand and he lost his grip.

Fall any distance and a person could risk permanent damage, but when trained for the fall, a man could walk away unharmed. The top of the brown four-door car met his back and ass with a painful crunch. The harsh cry that emerged from his throat wasn't planned, but he could no more stop it than he could stop moving. Because he never stopped moving. Rolling off the hood, he dropped to the pavement.

"Sphinx?"

Was that concern in the man's voice?

Fat chance of that.

The fucker.

Running in a crouch, he weaved in between cars and SUVs, slipping farther away from the threat.

Right about then, he wanted to stop but kept putting one foot in front of the other, hoping like hell he could get to the apartment before he passed out.

A few hours later and with some fancy hiding, he made it, but just barely.

When the door opened, he fell inward.

"Fucking hell!" Lex snarled and wrapped one burly arm around his waist to yank him inside and slam the door. "Were you followed?"

"No."

The big, beefy guy eyed him. "Leave a blood trail?"

"Don't think so."

He hissed when Lex shoved him toward the broken-down sofa. He gratefully sank onto the ripped cushions while Lex locked the deadbolt.

Lifting his shirt, Adam dabbed at the wound where the bullet nicked him. "It's just a crease."

Lex snorted and stomped into the kitchen and returned shortly with a first aid kit. Dropping the kit down, Lex nodded to his shirt.

"Take that off."

He did as he was told and used a wad of gauze to dab at the bloody wound. It was a lost cause and Lex was there again, pressing a clean towel to the injury.

"Here, hold this."

He held on, leaning his head against the back of the couch.

"So, did you talk to your contact at least?" Lex asked and kneeled down next to the couch. Concern flashed in Lex's cold, mud-colored eyes, but that was only because he was the guy's meal ticket. When a person lived on the fringes of society, beggars couldn't be choosers. Adam paid the rent for the tiny closet in the one-bedroom, overcrowded apartment.

"Does it look like I did?" he croaked, letting his lids slide shut.

He'd just close his eyes for one second. *Happy freaking birthday to me.*

Maybe then he'd wake up and this would all be a fucking dream.

One big nightmare.

CHAPTER TWO

Dalton

H E SLAMMED THROUGH THE METAL DOOR AND YANKED AT THE Velcro holding his tactical vest in place.

"My office, now," Ace snarled.

Dalton scowled toward the far end of the brightly lit room they called the bullpen to where his boss stood.

The man's big shoulders filled up the doorway to the office on the far side. Fluorescent lights flooded the room and a window that lined the wall near the top of the bullpen sent a smidge of light from the Southern California moon reflecting into the room. It was the only window they'd carved into the place, which was a bunker, really. All concealed beneath the Stone Ground Brewery.

Ace had told them gathering here was temporary. Yeah, and that had been several months ago. It no longer felt short-term. Truth be told, he didn't mind; the place Pegasus called headquarters was growing on him.

Tossing Mason, Gage, and the two FBI asshats a dark look, he stalked through the desks in the wide room and entered Ace's office. Reaching the far end of the large room, he dropped down into one of the vacant chairs that sat in front of his boss' wide oak desk after Ace took a seat behind it.

That they were meeting to debrief in Ace's office instead of the bullpen spoke volumes and he didn't have to wait long to hear why.

"Ventura County PD reported shots fired in the vicinity very near where you were," Ace growled at him, his booming voice cutting deep. And fuck if Dalton's stomach didn't sink a bit. "What happened to a peaceful meeting?"

Just fucking great. He squeezed his hands into fists and scowled. So much for staying under the radar of the local cops.

"Yeah, well," he said, jerking his head toward the two FBI agents who'd followed them into the room. "Those two clowns started shooting the minute Sphinx showed up."

"He's a wanted fugitive," FBI Agent Swather snarled, running a hand over his shiny black comb-over.

"That's right," Agent Sweenie said, backing up his partner, puffing out his chest in an attempt to look bigger.

Dalton scowled and Sweenie glanced away.

"Tweedle Dee and Tweedle Dum are out for blood," Dalton snapped.

Someone moved from the corner of the office, and Dalton had his weapon pulled out of his holster before the person even registered. Old habits from his military days kept him on his toes.

"Put that away," Ace ordered, and he tucked the gun back.

"You remember Agent Farnsworth," Ace continued.

Dalton squinted at the flat-faced, sixty-something, pudgy man with a mustache that curled over his top lip. The guy twisted the end of the hairs like he was some character from Sherlock Holmes, the wannabe motherfucker.

He gave the guy a dark look before turning back to Ace.

"You want Sphinx alive or dead?" he rasped.

"Dead," Farnsworth said.

"Alive," Ace snapped, throwing Farnsworth an annoyed look.

"Then next time, you might want to keep the team to in-house staff only," Dalton said.

Through the exchange, neither Mason nor Gage spoke a word, but he knew they felt the same. Pegasus worked well when they didn't have outside help, and after six fucking weeks of playing cat and mouse to a national traitor, Sphinx had finally agreed to a meeting. They'd even gotten close enough to exchange words. Albeit, the words were shouted, but that was a fuck ton closer than ever before. And it had all been for nothing.

"These two are more like hired guns than agents." He jerked his head to the FBI agents.

"Fuck you!" Sweenie snarled, still puffed up.

"You seemed to be in an awful hurry to kill him." Dalton's voice dripped with innuendos. "I wonder why that is?"

"Rein your man in or I'll do it for you," Farnsworth snapped at Ace.

And holy fuck was that the wrong thing to say to the boss.

Ace went still, much like a cobra would. His boss locked those silvery eyes on Farnsworth.

LETHAL

"Get the fuck out of my facility." The words were growled.

It took a moment for the order to register to the Special Agent-in-Charge and when they did, the man's face turned a deep shade of purple.

"This is my case! You were brought in because I was told you were the best." Farnsworth fisted his hands. "You can't fire me."

"Get out," Ace repeated, half rising from his chair.

"This is bullshit! You haven't heared the end of this," Farnsworth sputtered, tripping in his haste to back away from Ace.

"Tell it to the SecDef at your next luncheon," Ace said between clenched teeth with a tiny muscle ticking in his jaw.

After Farnsworth beat a hasty retreat, Ace slowly settled back in his chair.

"You two might as well join your boss," Dalton said to the other two FBI agents, beating Ace to it.

Sweenie and Swather stood, chairs crashing back. Both tossed angry glances their way before stomping out the door.

Gage shoved out of his chair and followed the three men out to the steps that would lead them to the entryway and back up to the brewery above. When it sounded like they weren't moving fast enough, Gage's deep voice rang out, "I'll shut the door after you."

Gage was the team's enforcer. Well, one of them, anyway. Typically, people left when Gage got in their faces and today was no exception.

Dalton turned his eyes back to Ace and held his boss's silvery gaze until the outer door closed and Gage resumed his seat in the office.

Mason, who'd been abnormally quiet so far, stood and

booted the office door shut with a crack before sprawling back in his chair.

"Fill me in," Ace ordered.

"We met at the place Sphinx suggested. Before we could get close, the two agents opened fire," he told Ace.

"Was Sphinx hit?"

Dalton rubbed his fingers over the hair on his jaw; he wore it too short for a beard, but too long for a full-on stubble. "I don't know."

"He was hit," Mason said.

"How do you know?" Dalton snapped his gaze to Mason.

"Blood on the railing at the apartment."

"We need to get Sphinx before the FBI kills him," Dalton responded, pulling a hand down his face. Something about the former CIA agent unsettled him. He rubbed at his chest through his shirt.

"We also need to find out what the hell is going on," Ace reminded them.

"We'd already have that information if we worked alone," Mason said, earning a hard look from their boss.

"Just saying." Mason shrugged.

"Don't say," Dalton growled.

Mason shot him a death glare, but fuck it, Mason was in enough trouble with Ace without popping off. The guy had gone off half-cocked on a few missions. Right now, though, Mason was keeping his wildness in check, but Dalton had a feeling it would only be a matter of time before Mason went off the rails. The guy was a hothead and not a team player.

Dalton wasn't much of a team player either, but he'd taken a job with Pegasus and would act accordingly. No sense in being a thorn in the team's side.

Ace was right, they needed to find out Sphinx's side of the story.

LETHAL

Ace caught his attention. "Can you reach out to him again?"

He let out a breath. It had taken weeks to get Sphinx to agree to a meeting—only to be shot at—so he was pretty sure the former agent wouldn't meet again.

"I can try. He probably won't respond."

"Let him know where you'll be," Ace suggested.

"And if he shows up and shoots me?"

"Wear a vest."

"I have a feeling he'll take a headshot." Dalton smirked at Ace.

Ace squinted. "You serious?"

"I don't know, but he's got to be pretty pissed," he said.

"If Sphinx sold that list, then he has no right to be pissed," Mason interjected. "He's got to know someone is coming for him."

The list Mason spoke of was filled with names from the intelligence community that included several US operatives and also assets. The only problem was that, according to ASAC Farnsworth, Sphinx's name was on the list he stole and sold.

Which posed the question: Why sell your own name to the enemy? Farnsworth's answer was that Sphinx must have deleted his name from the list before selling it. Dalton didn't buy it. There was also the fact that Sphinx had agreed to meet. Why agree to that if you're guilty? Shit didn't add up.

His phone buzzed with a silent reminder and he stared down at the calendar alert. *Adam's birthday*. He'd set the alert for yearly. Should he try to find Adam's new number and call? He nixed the thought the second it happened. Adam had changed his number, hence his desire not to be bothered. Not that the guy ever knew he'd called in the first place, but the bottom line was that Adam was happy, and it was best to leave him alone.

"See if Jacob can send Sphinx another message through that message board you used." Ace's voice jogged him back to the wide office and he nodded, tucking his phone and thoughts of Adam away.

Jacob Burns was the unit's technical genius. He'd been the one to find out how to contact Sphinx in the first place. Dalton shoved from his chair and filed to the door along with Mason and Gage, but before stepping through, he paused.

Usually, when someone stole secrets, the government wanted the guy caught to get information. Important information, like who Sphinx sold the list to. This didn't seem to be the case. The FBI wanted Sphinx eliminated, and that bugged the shit out of him.

"Do you know why the FBI wants Sphinx dead?"

"Selling secrets isn't enough?"

"Is it?" he countered and walked out, leaving Ace looking thoughtful.

So, according to the FBI, Sphinx was a traitor of the worst kind. Only, Pegasus had been given one side of the story. Sphinx's side had yet to be heard. And after tonight's shitshow, he may never know Sphinx's side. Dalton hated the lack of information. It felt like going in blind and sounded sketchy as fuck. This whole thing felt off.

And when shit felt off, he made it his business to find out what the fuck was going on.

And he would find out, one way or another.

CHAPTER THREE

Adam

DALTON *FUCKING* WEBER.

Of all the assholes to run into, it had to be him.

Dalton had been labeled as being one of the most dangerous men on the planet. Adam knew that because he'd been following Dalton's career for years. The ex-Marine was a former Raider, which was the equivalent of Army Special Forces with a few major differences during wartime missions.

Dalton had turned mercenary for hire for a few years after serving and then fell off the radar. When the fuck had Dalton gone to work for the Feds?

Hell, Adam now felt lucky he'd walked away still breathing.

Easing up on the side of the bed, he swung his legs over and sat up. Clutching his side, the room whirled a bit and he steadied himself with a grip on the musty-smelling mattress.

At some point last night, he'd made it to his bed after eating something and checking his email.

He blinked around at the old, bare paneling on the wall. The room was a closet, really. Lex and Splicer had turned it into a place he could sleep. And after thinking of his roommate, Splicer appeared in the doorway.

"Thinking of me?"

"How do you do that?" Adam frowned.

"I heard the box springs creaking." The thin, long-haired man grunted and held out a bottle of water. The fingers of Splicer's other hand tapped against his leg and his gaze darted around.

Adam took the container, cracked the cap off, and guzzled the whole thing.

"I take it the meeting didn't go as planned?"

"They shot me, so no."

"What now?"

What now? Now, he needed to get out of there and away from his current set of roomies. He suspected that one or both Lex and Splicer weren't on his side. Call it a gut feeling, but he always trusted his gut.

"One of the men after me happens to be an old friend of my brother."

"I thought your family was dead?"

He'd never told Splicer that little fact. That the guy knew kind of solidified Splicer was researching him. For money? Probably. What he didn't know was why he hadn't been arrested if Splicer and Lex were selling him out. He suspected it had to do with both men wanting to get as much money out of him as they could before they ratted him out. Maybe they were waiting for orders. Some would call him crazy, but he believed in keeping your friends close and your enemies closer. That gave him about two days tops.

Adam nodded. "They are. But dead or not, it doesn't mean they didn't have friends." He shoved slowly up from the bed. His side was tender, but all and all, it could have been a lot worse.

"Who's this guy?"

"Guy?" Adam frowned.

"Your brother's friend?"

Grabbing a button-down shirt from the cardboard box in the corner, he shrugged it on. He was reluctant to name Dalton.

"Oh, just some asshole."

"Well, this asshole shot at you. I doubt they're interested in what you have to say now," Splicer said, crossing his restless arms against his thin chest.

Adam squinted, buttoned up the shirt he wore, and finger-combed his hair. "They reached out to *me*."

"So that's that?"

"Maybe," Adam lied.

There was no maybe about it. No way in hell was he taking a backseat on this. He needed to find out who had blacklisted him as a traitor.

It had to be related to the list he'd found.

If he could find out who gave the order to kill him, it might be his ticket back into the agency.

The message on the board had assured him Pegasus had answers. That was a lie. The message had been a setup to lure him into a trap. They didn't want to hear his side of the story—they wanted him dead.

"You should lay low." Splicer moved back when he approached the door. "I mean, they shot you, man."

"There is that." He studied the former DEA agent. Splicer had been fired from the police force after money and drugs had gone missing during a bust. He'd taken a plea deal and served a nickel.

These guys had come recommended via Adam's former handler, who assured him nobody would look for him at Splicer's pad.

But now he wasn't so sure about the guy and he damned well wasn't sure about Lex. Splicer and Lex both knew too much about his situation.

"How much longer can you put me up?"

"As long as you can pay the rent."

The cash he had on him wouldn't rent a hotel room, much less cover the cost of the closet. The streets it was, then. He'd lived on them before.

"Give me a couple of days and I'll be out."

Splicer squinted, pulling at the hairs on his bushy beard. "You don't need to run just yet."

"Yeah, I do."

"Why don't you turn yourself in?"

"And what? Sit in a prison cell until someone comes to kill me?" he bit out. "No thanks. I'll take my chances on the street."

"They reached out again," Lex said from where he sat at the dirty table. Fast food wrappers and food-filled plates cluttered the scratched surface in the smoke-filled room. Lex had cleared a small space for Adam's laptop.

"How'd you get my password?"

"You left it open." Lex shrugged and scratched at his exposed stomach.

Gritting his teeth, Adam approached the tiny square kitchen.

Fuck. He rubbed his head, his brain foggy. Had he left his laptop open after checking his email? He must have been out of it more than he'd realized last night.

Or maybe, Lex had spied on him while he was out of it.

Stay on your own and there'd be nobody to snoop and steal, he silently reminded himself.

The site Lex was speaking of was on the dark web, the messages encrypted, so Lex wouldn't be able to see the words. All Lex would see was that Adam had gotten an alert.

The hacker who was sending the messages on the dark web was insanely good. So good, in fact, that he knew it couldn't be Dalton. It had to be someone on Dalton's team. As his memory recalled, Dalton hadn't liked using computers.

That was about fifteen years ago when Adam had been eighteen and Dalton twenty-three. Maybe things had changed? That had been a lifetime ago. Adam doubted it, though.

"Let me see." He took his laptop from in front of Lex, saving it from the ashes hanging from the man's cigarette. Carrying his computer to the couch, he sat cross-legged and clicked through the website, finding the new message.

"Sorry for the hassle S. Meet me again. I'll be good. D."

His lip curled at the S. It stood for Sphinx, a handle he'd earned while working with the agency. It was better than the nickname of Cupcake Dalton had called him when they'd first met. He'd hated it and returned the favor by calling Dalton the big bad wolf.

Well, he had news for Dalton, he wasn't a cupcake any longer even though Dalton may still be a big bad wolf. The only difference between them was their size. He could never match Dalton's larger frame, but Adam was hella fast and not many came even close to catching him.

The Army had turned him ripcord lean, but not even the military could make him Dalton's height.

Signing in via the back door of a search engine, it took him several long minutes to get into the website he needed.

Now that he knew Dalton was behind this, or a part of this, he needed more information.

Dalton Weber, age thirty-eight, six feet five inches. His tattoos were too numerous to list, but Adam had studied each and every one of them up close and personal. It looked like there were a lot more of them and he wondered what else they covered...

Concentrate!

He clenched his teeth and clicked past the military information. He knew all that. While Dalton had picked up mercenary work after his discharge in 2008, Adam, on the other hand, had gone into the Army before joining the CIA. The agency had been what caused him trouble, but he aimed to correct that.

The next few pages were sparse with large sections blacked out. It was going to be hard getting data on what Dalton had been up to. It took several more minutes to come across the words *Top Secret* and *Pegasus*. He'd heard of Pegasus; they were almost the equivalent of Phoenix. Both were elite groups that stepped in when law enforcement's hands were tied, with one big difference. Phoenix followed the law, while Pegasus ran in deeper, darker circles. They could make people disappear like vapor.

Pegasus, though...could they help him? Should he trust Dalton with his real identity?

Fuck no. Dalton could suck a dick. That didn't mean Adam wasn't willing to meet again, and now that he knew it was Dalton, nothing would keep him from fucking with the man.

He sent back a response to the dark web message. *Check your email.*

It took him another few seconds to set up a dummy

email account and send Dalton a note. Afterward, he deleted the account and closed his laptop.

Slipping out the apartment door, he found a seat on the stairs and tugged out a burner phone he'd picked up the day before but had yet to use.

His call was unanswered, and a machine picked up at the other end.

"Last color of the day: green. Operative 2564, requesting a callback," he said and hung up.

Two seconds later, the phone rang.

"Sphinx?" Relief swept through Adam at the sound of his handler's voice. Although Richard Black knew his identity, they always used code names over the airwaves.

"Any word on who's behind this?"

"Not yet." Regret filled Black's worried voice. "Just lay low."

"I have been," Adam said through his teeth.

"I need more time to figure out what the hell is going on and who the hell is involved."

"I think my location has been compromised," he said.

"Is there anywhere else you can go?" Black asked. His handler knew he couldn't just use a CIA safe house; the agencies would be all over his ass in seconds. He needed to stay free until Black caught whoever the hell had leaked the list and blamed him.

"Yeah, I know someone," Adam said.

"Sphinx?"

"Yeah?"

"Stay safe."

He hung up and sat holding the phone before he punched in a phone number he hadn't called in years and waited while it rang.

"Hello?"

"Mrs. Weber?"

"Yes, who's this?"

"It's Adam."

There was a short moment where he heard her gasp of surprise.

"Oh, my goodness! Adam, sweetie, it's so good to hear from you." Dalton's mom, Leslie, always made him feel like one of the family. And for five years, he had been. In fact, he'd thought that he'd be with them forever, but then he'd gone and fallen for Dalton and ruined everything.

"I was so sorry to hear about Randy." Her voice softened.

"Thank you."

"I wanted to come to the funeral but it's so hard for me to travel in the winter, and I'd caught pneumonia that year," she said, her voice filled with worry.

"It's okay, your health comes first."

Randy had been buried in the hills of Kentucky. It was a place where his brother had wanted to settle down and start a life. Somewhere away from the harsh memories of his Alaskan childhood. Adam couldn't blame his brother for relocating there several years ago. Randy had numerous friends in Kentucky and Adam had invited them to celebrate Randy's life. What he hadn't expected was for Dalton to show up.

"How are you?" Leslie always thought about others first.

A lump grew in his throat. "I'm good. How's your family doing? Tell me everything."

It may have been underhanded, but sometimes people had to use desperate measures when their lives were at stake. His question was all it took, and she launched into a nonstop barrage of stories about her husband and children.

And God help him, he drank up every single word.

CHAPTER FOUR

Dalton

HE'D WAITED ALL THE NEXT DAMNED DAY, THEN FINALLY, SPHINX had responded.

The meeting was on again.

Tomorrow night.

Sandhill Junkyard,

11 PM, come alone, S.

He'd been worried the fuck up with the FBI had scared Sphinx away.

Scared wasn't the right word, but the man was cagey. There was something oddly intriguing about the guy. Dalton shook it off. He was nothing more than a job. Sphinx was elusive as hell and it kind of reminded Dalton of himself. That was all.

He'd like to sit down and pick the guy's brain apart and see what made him tick. Starting with: why had Sphinx stolen that list? Who had he sold it to and why did the FBI want him dead?

Scrolling through his phone, his finger hovered over Adam's phone number. The phone number was new, well, a few years old at least, but Dalton had done some underhanded things to get it. He closed his phone without dialing. Was Adam happy? Did he have the white picket-fenced life he'd always wanted?

A noise from one of the bunker's backrooms pulled him from his funk, and he glanced at the darkness through the slice of windows.

One more day to wait for Sphinx. He might as well wrap it up for the night and get a fresh start in the morning.

"Dalton?"

"What's up?" He tucked his phone away and swiveled in his chair to find Jacob Burns standing there. The techie's dark hair hung over bright eyes.

Reaching his desk, Jacob placed a folder on the dark wood in front of him.

"I found him after he signed on to a website I've been monitoring. It took a while," Jacob said, shaking the hair from his face.

Dalton glanced at the folder and then back up. "Who did you find?"

"Sphinx. And that's his IP address and a copy of the file he was searching for."

"Seriously?"

Jacob grinned. "No, I'm lying."

"Okay, smartass," he huffed.

"I wasn't able to get the exact location because he logged off, but that's the apartment building. Have fun finding him." Jacob waggled his fingers at him, and his tall, lean form disappeared down the hall toward the communications room.

Dalton picked up the folder and flipped it open.

"What are you smiling about?"

He tossed the folder down and swiveled in his chair to face his best friend.

"This Sphinx guy," he said to Eagle and flicked a finger at the file.

Declan Weller, code-named Eagle, lifted the folder from the desk and sprawled in the chair across from him before flipping it open. "This is your military record." Eagle's gaze flew to meet his.

"It is."

"Sphinx was looking into you?"

"Apparently."

"Is this his IP address?" Eagle tossed the file back on the desk.

"Yeah. The location is sketchy, but it's worth a shot. Want to come with me?"

"That you would have to ask." Eagle grinned and shoved up out of his chair.

Dalton laughed and grabbed his truck keys. He should have known Eagle would come with him. They'd gone to junior high together and even when Eagle had moved away, Dalton had kept in touch with the man through the years. When Eagle had joined the Army instead of the Marines, Dalton hadn't held it against him.

When Dalton had become a mercenary after the Marines, Eagle never judged him. His friend would call out of the blue whenever Eagle had leave. Eagle was one of those friends that a person could go years without seeing but when together, it felt like no time had passed.

He and Eagle entered the weapons room and Dalton pulled on his vest and checked his weapon.

"Where are you two headed?" Lincoln Beckett, also known as Link, asked upon coming into the tactical room.

"IP address of a possible Sphinx sighting," Eagle said, slamming a clip into his Glock. "Wanna come?"

"Need me to?" Link asked and leaned a hip against the lockers.

"Never."

Link rolled his eyes at Eagle's snarky comeback and opened a locker to pull on a vest and check his weapon.

"Hey guys," Mason said from the open doorway. "The NSA is also after Sphinx."

"What are you talking about?" Dalton scowled at Mason and the man looked away.

"We'll be lucky to catch this guy alive," Link muttered, slamming a clip into his sidearm.

"You knew about the NSA?" Dalton advanced on Mason.

"Yes." Mason's chin tipped upward and Dalton was tempted to knock him on his ass.

"Then why the hell didn't you say something earlier?" he growled on his approach.

"Because it was on a need-to-know basis and you didn't need to know," Mason responded.

He caught Mason by the shirt and fisted the material. The man's back bumped the locker and the door rattled.

It wasn't a fair fight.

For Dalton.

Mason was out of his hold and delivering a kidney punch that Dalton barely blocked before he could even fucking blink. Still, though, Mason bounced away and put a good distance between them. Dalton's hands squeezed closed.

"Knock it off," Ace's deep voice boomed from the doorway.

Dalton stared at Mason, who stared right back. "Don't keep information from us," Dalton growled.

"Dalton, Mason came to correct his lack of sharing," Ace responded.

"He had a shot in your office yesterday and all fucking day today to come clean," Dalton charged right back.

Mason's teeth snapped and he sucked in a deep breath and then deflated. "Sorry. Trust comes…slowly."

He squinted at the small, fair-haired man who moved faster than anyone he'd ever met; well, except maybe Sphinx.

"Get over yourself," Dalton said slowly. "We're all here to do a job. If you don't trust us, then maybe you shouldn't be here."

Nobody spoke, not even Ace, and the room went strangely quiet.

Dalton didn't give a flying fuck and held Mason's gaze; he could see the wheels turning in that bright head of his, and after a moment, Mason slowly nodded. He figured that meant the guy was on board.

"Grab your gear," he told Mason.

After one startled look at still being included, Mason hurried to gear up.

Ace sent him a smirking smile of gratitude and he gave his boss a brief nod.

Dalton was known for his peacekeeping abilities, but don't fuck with him about stupid shit because he'd call people on it every damned time.

After their last lieutenant retired, Dalton had been promoted, and he took his job as second-in-command very fucking seriously.

Sliding behind the wheel of one of the team's black SUVs, Eagle jumped in the front passenger seat.

"All buckled up?" Eagle tossed a grin over his shoulder.

"Ass," Link muttered, snapping his belt with a click.

Dalton wasn't worried about Link and Eagle—they went way back. The pair had served together in a Special Forces unit known as Fury. Those two were best friends and in sync, almost like they could read each other's minds. Inseparable, they'd joined Pegasus a few months before him.

Dalton had later learned that Eagle had dropped his name to Ace when their boss had been on the search for a new lieutenant. Dalton had found out later that neither Holden nor Beckett Wreck had wanted the job. The pair were the only two missing from the unit at the moment. Right now, they were traveling across Europe with their adopted kids.

"Have you heard from Beckett or Holden?" he asked Eagle.

"Yeah, they made it to Italy," Eagle said.

"Thought they were heading to Austria," Link said.

"That too." Eagle snapped his seatbelt in place.

"From what Ace said, we'll be one short in the field when they do get back, Beckett needs additional time off," Dalton said.

"I hear Jacob wants to be in the field," Eagle said and tossed him a look.

"What a waste," Mason muttered. "He's a technical genius."

He shot Mason a stern look in the rearview mirror as he took the freeway onramp. "There's nothing wrong with doing both."

"I know a guy, his name is Seth Grayson. Works for Phoenix in the field. Used to be known as Reboot Hell," Link said.

Phoenix was a mirror unit to Pegasus that worked out of Northern California—they all reported to the same chief.

"No shit?" Mason gaped at Link.

"No shit." Link smirked and tried to rub his knuckles on Mason's hair, but the man slapped Link's hand away.

"I'm not a fucking kid."

"Look like one," Eagle laughed at Mason.

Mason flipped Eagle the middle finger.

"Knock it off," Dalton told Eagle. "Do something useful and get the file from my bag and find something about Sphinx we don't already know."

Eagle tugged out the folder from the duffel bag and flipped it open.

"Six feet tall, brown hair, blue eyes. The name is blacked out. CIA says that's classified."

"Don't you think that's weird?" Dalton asked.

"Think Jacob could find out?" Eagle tossed him a look.

"I've had Jacob on it," Dalton confirmed. "So far, he's gotten nowhere."

"Everything here refers to him as Sphinx." Eagle held up a piece of paper to the fading light in the cab. "Looks like his first name might start with an F or that could be an A. Maybe a B?" Eagle shoved the paper back into the folder.

"You know how these agencies are," Dalton said with a glance to Mason. "You think you can get the name?"

After all, Mason was former CIA.

Mason shook his head. "I already tried. Nothing is listed but his code name."

"What about you?" Link asked Mason. "Were you listed?"

"Only as Mason."

"I'm going to keep Jacob on it. It's worth a try," Dalton muttered.

• • •

The street appeared in darkened silence and Dalton sat for a few moments before removing the keys from the ignition and quietly exiting the vehicle.

The rest of his team eased the SUV's doors shut and gathered around him.

He eyed the apartment complex located one block down.

"That's going to be fun," Eagle murmured and nodded at the large multilevel building.

"Yeah, fan out." He kept his voice low.

"I'll take the back," Mason quietly offered.

"I'll go with," Link told Mason.

"You don't think Sphinx knows we're here?" Eagle frowned.

"Maybe. Stay out of sight," Dalton said.

"He's a Sphinx, he knows," Mason grumbled.

"Right. A Sphinx. And don't forget, he's fast," Dalton reminded the men.

"And smart," Eagle pointed out like that was something he didn't already know.

Smart was putting it mildly. Sphinx was too fucking smart for his own good. And Dalton wanted him…wanted to catch him like he wanted nothing else on earth. His obsession wasn't normal, but fuck it. He wanted to catch the man every agency wanted. Catching the FBI's most wanted would be a commendation to put on his shelf.

Is that the only reason? He shoved the annoying voice away. It was a need to catch the guy, plain and simple, and nothing more.

Anticipation tightened his gut.

CHAPTER FIVE

Adam

He wanted to laugh at their conversation, but that would have given his position away.

What part about the junkyard tomorrow night did Dalton not understand? It certainly didn't mean to show up at his place with backup a day early.

But his bigger problem was that his location shouldn't have gotten out.

It was his own fault.

He hadn't discovered the spyware until last night, and only after he'd searched for Dalton's name and info on the internet.

Still woozy from his injury, he'd finally noticed something funky about his computer.

Upon further inspection, someone—and he was putting

his money on Dalton's crew—had been able to remotely access his laptop and he'd fucking missed it.

He felt off his game. He'd missed something as simple as a damned hack because he'd been too preoccupied with Dalton.

Right away, he had wiped his laptop and powered it off, but by that time, it had been too late.

Lex or Splicer had fucked with his computer, making it vulnerable to hackers. And it had been done deliberately.

Tired as hell, he had waited one more night to leave. He had lain on the lumpy mattress, holding his gun, with one eye open.

He had listened to every creak of the rickety old building. Early this morning, he'd acted as if nothing was wrong. All day long, he kept an ear tuned to every sound. Splicer avoided his gaze and Lex tossed him frowns; Adam ignored them both.

As evening approached, he headed to the closet and had begun to pack his things. Leaving under the cover of darkness was the plan.

"You don't need to leave." Splicer had followed him and stood in the small doorway.

"Yeah, I do." He shoved the rest of his stuff, which wasn't much, inside his backpack and slipped it over his shoulders.

"Stay at least another day," Lex spoke up from his spot on the worn couch.

"Nah, I'm good. I appreciate everything, though," he said and didn't miss the way Splicer and Lex glanced at each other.

Before they could voice further objections or do something stupid like preventing him from leaving, he walked out the door and up the stairs instead of down.

Sure enough, the door opened and Splicer ran down the stairs, Lex following, holding a gun.

LETHAL

Amateurs. He rolled his eyes and made his way to the roof.

He'd slept beneath the stars before; he could do it again. He'd waited an hour or so before making his way down and outside, only to find that destiny seemed to be playing with him.

Which brought him to his current predicament: Dalton and his men.

A slight movement from his left jogged him back from the man who consumed too much of his thoughts.

Adam plastered himself against the apartment wall when two men slipped right past him. One was big and the other small. He paid them no mind. His eyes locked on Dalton's wide shoulders in the distance.

Go, his inner voice kept telling him, but he stayed still.

Did he want to take a chance on Dalton?

Fuck, he'd crushed hard over his brother's friend. The big badass older Dalton had been his younger self's dream man and he'd spent a few years following his brother and Dalton around like a lost puppy.

Until the day Dalton had crushed all of his fantasies. He shoved the thought away. Like hell he'd go back down that dead-end road. Those days of following Dalton around were long fucking gone now.

Even the memory of the man's kisses had begun to fade.

Right, keep telling yourself that, he scowled.

It *had* all faded. Well, until the second he'd heard Dalton's deep voice, and then the memories had come rushing back.

Regardless of their past, Dalton clearly hadn't recognized him. To be fair, he had been wearing a beanie pulled down over his face with only the mouth and eyes cut out.

A noise snapped him out of his distraction and he held his breath. *Get it fucking together. Walk the fuck away.*

But damn it. He wanted answers. He needed to know who the hell had set him up.

Maybe, just maybe Dalton had answers. *Since when have you ever needed anyone's help getting information, much less his?* Never, but there was always a first time. Slipping through the shadows, he waited until Dalton came up the narrow sidewalk to the apartment building.

Adam eased out, careful to remain mostly in the shadows and out of the direct area lights that were positioned around the apartment building. Balanced on the balls of his feet, he stayed ready to disappear.

Dalton stopped abruptly at his appearance, gazing at him from across the distance. It was as if Dalton were trying to make out his face and eyes, but Adam knew the mask gave nothing away.

"Feel like talking?"

Adam tipped his head to the side, gauging the soft warmth in the man's rumbling voice. It had a come-hither quality that made a person dream of strong arms and hard kisses. It also reminded him of what they'd lost when Dalton had walked away like a fucking coward. Old anger came rushing up.

One part of him wanted to take a chance on Dalton. Maybe just exchange a few words and see how that went. Dalton's team was already inside the apartment building and they *were* alone. The other part of him wanted to tell the man to fuck off, but that wouldn't solve anything.

He slowly took a step farther out into the area light.

A snap and crunch of gravel beneath a shoe had his heart slamming into his chest.

Snick, snick, snick.

The bricks exploded near his head. In a blink, he flew backward, melting into the darkness. One bullet had come so close, a piece of brick had popped against his beanie. *Fuck this!*

"Stop shooting!" Dalton hollered, sounding furious.

LETHAL

He didn't wait for whoever it was to take the kill shot. Disappearing between overgrown shrubs, he crouched, eyes locked on the men trying to kill him. Fucking suits.

"You let him get away!" one of the suits snapped, waving a gun.

Dalton stalked up to the suit and punched him in the nose, knocking him to the ground. "You son of a bitch!"

"You just assaulted an agent!" The guy lunged up from the ground and charged Dalton.

Dalton caught and swung the guy around with a fist in his jacket, but the agent hung on and gave a few weak punches. Suddenly, both the big and smaller men Adam had seen earlier and another even bigger guy—all pulled the agent from Dalton.

Adam didn't stop to see the finish of the fight. Dalton and his goons could go fuck themselves. He tore down the walkway, his shoes silent on the cement.

Reaching where he had stashed his backpack, he slipped it on and clung to the shadows. Walking quickly out of the area, Adam vanished like vapor.

Obviously, Dalton was in with the FBI.

Then why did he tell the guy to stop shooting? Why did Dalton punch the agent in the nose? Fuck if he knew, and he wasn't waiting around to ask.

Being blacklisted had been devastating, and his kindhearted handler had been tapped out. The vision of Richard Black's weathered face, lined with worry when he couldn't help him, drew a lump to Adam's throat. Black had twin boys and a beautiful wife. Adam had spent several holidays with Black and his family since he hadn't ever gone back home.

At least this encounter answered one question—he sure the hell wouldn't be meeting with Dalton at the junkyard tomorrow night. He'd bet money Dalton would bring his goons and the FBI.

Screw this.

His temple pounded and his left side hurt like hell, the wound not even starting to heal. He needed a place—a safe place—to recuperate.

And Dalton? Dalton had had his chance and he'd blown it.

Adam would take his chances elsewhere.

Everyone thought he had taken a list of operatives. Only it wasn't a list of operatives. It was a list of people being on the take—high-powered people being paid off to look the other way when sensitive information was leaked.

He would take the flash drive to the highest government official he could find. The highest trustworthy official.

Just who that was, he didn't know, but he would find someone. Not everyone in the government was corrupt. What about the Secretary of Defense? He'd heard about the man's integrity through the grapevine. Only he couldn't do that because Pegasus reported to the SecDef.

And Pegasus had turned on him.

He couldn't go to anyone remotely connected to Pegasus, the FBI, or the CIA for that matter. His only hope was to hold out for Black to find out who'd burned him.

He wracked his brain for someone else he could reach out to but came up with nothing.

Sometimes, being an orphan had its drawbacks. Of course, when he'd joined the CIA, it had worked in his favor, but now that he was blacklisted, his orphan status felt like a noose around his neck.

He could call his ex. He crushed that thought the second it came up. Michael hated his guts and Adam didn't blame the guy, not after the way he'd left things.

So here he was, a burned spy with no one to count on and nothing to his name. The FBI had frozen his bank accounts, converged on his apartment before he could get back in, and they'd taken his vehicle. They'd left him with only his wits.

He'd hadn't known what he was going to do until he'd heard Leslie's soft, soothing voice. Breaking down, he'd asked to borrow money. Tugging out his phone, he logged into the new account he'd set up that morning under a bogus name. The funds had come through. Staring at the large amount, his chest grew tight.

Dalton's mom had been the closest thing to a mother he'd ever known and as guilty as he felt, it didn't stop him from scheduling a flight.

CHAPTER SIX

Dalton

THE NEXT MORNING, HE DIDN'T WAIT FOR ACE TO CALL HIM TO his office but instead, walked over and leaned a shoulder against the doorjamb.

Ace took one look at his face, pushed away the laptop he was typing on, and leaned back in his chair.

Something in his face made Ace's mouth draw into a flat line.

"Shut the door," his boss rasped.

He shut the door and took a seat before filling Ace in on the shit show that had happened at the apartment complex and how he'd come close to strangling an agent the night before.

"I had the men sweep the SUV for bugs before sending them home last night. They found one beneath the fucking bumper."

"Farnsworth was pissed enough to follow you." Ace rubbed a hand over his beard.

Dalton nodded and raked his fingers through his hair. "Sphinx wants to talk, I can feel it, but the FBI wants him dead," he finished flatly.

Silence filled the office. Ace squinted and then lifted the phone and punched in a number; it rang over the speaker. An administrative assistant answered the line and insisted that the Secretary of Defense couldn't possibly come to the phone.

"I don't care what he's doing. If you want to keep your job, you'll tell him Cohen Gray is on the phone right the fuck now," Ace told the man.

"One moment."

Music filled the speaker and Dalton held his boss' silvery gaze in silence.

Less than a minute later, the line was picked up.

The Secretary's deep voice came over the line. "Ace, what's wrong?"

"Dave, we have a problem." Ace gave Dave the shortened version of the events over the past week.

"Son of a bitch."

It warmed something in his chest that the SecDef took this shit as seriously as they did.

"You think ASAC Farnsworth is in on this?"

"He wants Sphinx dead," Dalton said before Ace could answer. "Which is damned odd if we're trying to find out who Sphinx sold that list to," he finished.

"If that doesn't sound like shit in a pile, I don't know what does," Ace added.

"God damned incompetent..." Dave growled.

"Dave?" Ace said.

"What?"

"Have you seen the list of assets and operatives Sphinx stole?"

There was a long moment of silence and then a low sigh came over the line. "No, I haven't and I wouldn't. It's not something I'm privy to."

Which made sense because of the sensitive nature of the list.

"Has the FBI ensured everyone on that list is protected?" Ace tapped a pen on his desktop.

"I don't know," Dave said with a sigh.

"Is there anyone in the FBI you can trust?" Dalton shot out.

He earned a dark look from Ace because let's face it, not everyone in the agency was bad, but he'd bet his last fucking dollar that Farnsworth and his goons were bad seeds.

"FBI Director Scott is a close friend of mine. Hell, he's the reason you're involved. He needed a favor, so he owes me."

"Can you reach out to him?" Ace asked.

"Yeah, I will. Scott will have Farnsworth's head on a pike if he's running around with guns blazing. I'll see if Scott has issued an order to protect those people on the list," Dave said and then asked, "Has Sphinx dropped off the grid?"

"I was supposed to meet him tomorrow night, but I doubt he'll show up now that he's been shot at twice on my watch," Dalton said.

"See if you can reach out to him. When you meet him, tell him that I'll get to the bottom of this shit. To come in and we'll talk," the SecDef said.

"We will," Ace said. "If he won't agree to a meet, we'll see if he will at least try to communicate via email."

"Okay. Take care, you two. Have a good holiday. I'll be in touch."

The line went dead and Ace punched the end call button.

"Christmas is only a week away," Ace reminded him. "I promised to close the office for two weeks."

"I know. They haven't had a break in months. Let them go home. I can handle contacting Sphinx."

Ace nodded. "Sounds good, and I'll call you the minute Dave gets back to me."

Dalton headed out of the office and toward his own desk, which was part of the bullpen area where they all had desks. The office was looking scarce. Most of Pegasus's employees were either on assignments, in the field, or had already left for holiday plans.

"All good?" Eagle asked from the desk next to his.

"Maybe?" Dalton sprawled in his own chair and pulled his laptop closer.

"What now?" Link quietly asked from his spot sprawled in a chair across from Eagle's desk.

Mason came inside and shut the door before coming over to sit on the edge of Dalton's desk. "So now what?" Mason unknowingly echoed Link.

"Go home." He waved them off.

"It's only nine o'clock." Mason made a face.

"It's Christmas next week," he muttered. "You're not even supposed to be here."

"Yes!" Eagle pumped his fist in the air, earning an eye roll from Link. "What? I love pumpkin pie." Eagle grinned at Link.

Link made a face. "Leave the pecan to me."

"Fine, but I'm driving," Eagle retorted.

"No, you're not," Link said.

"Wanna bet?" Eagle laughed and shoved away from his desk.

"Happy holidays, you two," Dalton said, and the pair waved and wandered off.

He eyed Mason. "What are your plans?"

"Forest and Greene are buying a huge tree and we're all gathering over at their house." Mason spoke of his brother and brother-in-law, who didn't live far from the Pegasus facility. In fact, Greene used to be the second-in-command of Pegasus prior to the birth of his daughter. Having three kids and a new baby had given Greene a new perspective on life, and now the man did full-time consulting work.

"Have fun," he told Mason.

"You want to come? One more person in a group of twenty won't make a difference," Mason said.

"Nah, I'm good, but thanks." He hadn't been home for Christmas in a long time, and going to someone else's house instead of home to see his own family didn't sit well with him

"Okay, see ya. Don't work too hard." Mason left and the room became quiet except for the whirl of the heater kicking on. California or not, December was cold and he was glad for the warmth.

Dalton turned his attention to his laptop. He hated the damned thing, but out of necessity, he'd learned how to work one over the past decade.

First, he sent a message to the last known email address of Sphinx. As he suspected, the message came back undeliverable.

He brought up the dark web via the directions Jacob had given him and typed a message and then deleted it and then typed another one. And deleted that one. It went on like that for several more times before he finally settled on something simple.

S, what a complete blunder. It won't happen again. Still hope we're on for the junkyard. D.

CHAPTER SEVEN

Adam

Nobody thought twice about Adam Smith catching a flight from LAX to Fairbanks, Alaska.

It was one of the aliases he'd kept from the CIA. It was only to be used in emergencies, and this was one.

Yet, the closer he got to Fairbanks, the more he regretted coming. More than being here, he regretted borrowing the money. He shouldn't have come. He should be anywhere *but* here. What the fuck had he been thinking?

Standing in the freezing cold without a coat, he gripped his backpack and turned back toward the inside of the airport. He must have been out of his mind. Of all the stupid things he'd done, this was one of them.

"Adam!"

He whirled around at the sound of his name and found Dalton's younger sister, Mary, rushing toward him. Before he could even open his arms, she'd closed both of hers around his waist and hugged him tightly. He hung on as her flowery perfume and warmth engulfed him. Of all the Weber clan, he was the closest to Mary. All the memories of their exploits came flooding back. She'd been the one to encourage him to go after Dalton.

"I couldn't believe it when mom said you were coming home. And for Christmas, too!" She kissed his cheek, linked her arm with his, and pulled him toward a waiting minivan.

Mary opened the middle passenger-side door and he was ushered inside before he could say a word. The seats were leather and warmed his ass, and the interior held that new car smell. A shudder swept through his chest and his throat squeezed as he fumbled with the seatbelt.

"You poor thing, you're freezing!" Mary pulled a thick, heavy blanket from the back and spread it out over his lap even before he was completely buckled in.

The inside of the van was filled with people who took turns hugging him even if it was a bit awkward due to the seating. Dalton's other sister, Renee, hugged him just as tightly as Mary had. Dalton's younger brother, Colton, sat behind the wheel and turned, giving him a huge grin, and offered his fist. Leaning forward, he returned the man's fist bump.

"About time you came home," Colton said and eased the large van away from the airport curb after Mary shut the sliding door.

Dalton's mom, Leslie, came out of the front passenger seat and knelt in the aisle in front of him to bear hug him. He leaned over and wrapped his arms around her. She smelled like cookies, and he pictured her baking his favorite, chocolate chip. His throat closed again and he swallowed and blinked his eyes, hoping not to embarrass himself.

LETHAL

"I'm so freaking glad you're here," she whispered near his ear.

"Mom, language." Renee laughed. "Sensitive ears here."

"Oh poo!" Leslie released him with a smile and sat back on her heels. "Freaking isn't cursing. Tell them, Adam. Plus, I'm allowed to curse if I want. Besides, your father isn't here."

He waited for Renee's comeback. Of all the kids to argue with their mom, Renee came first.

"Dad curses more than you do, Mom," Renee pointed out with one hand rubbing at her swollen belly.

His mouth dropped open when he got his first full glimpse of her.

Renee's smile was a mile long. "Yep. Eight months." She ignored his shock and took his hand to place it on her very pregnant belly. "This will be our second one."

"I didn't even know you had one, much less two," he croaked, cupping his hand around the mound.

"Yeah," Renee said softly. "Jenny will be two in February."

"I've missed so much," he murmured, easing back in his seat.

"It's okay, baby," Leslie said and cupped his cheek. "We will fill you in on everything."

"Mom, please get in your seat," Colton warned, and Leslie finally scooted back and climbed in the passenger seat to buckle up.

"I want to hear it all," Adam said in a wobbling voice.

"And don't you worry about *you know who*, I'll handle him," Leslie said with a tip of her chin.

Laughter and giggles rang out inside the van.

It might appear odd to hear a mother call her own son *"you know who,"* but they'd done it for years. Keeping secrets was a Weber family art. Dalton was much like his father,

43

serious and levelheaded, and the rest of the family did their damnedest to keep those two out of the loop.

Leslie tipped her blonde head and the bun at her nape shifted. The rest of the clan's hair ranged from light to dark. With Mary and Renee both light brown, Colton was blond like his mother and Dalton was dark-haired like his father.

Wisps of hair had escaped from Leslie's bun, creating a halo around her head. *Like an angel*, he thought, but she was one tough angel and ruled her family, even Dalton, like nobody's business. She was all about treating people with respect as long as they deserved it. Her motto, and one she'd taught him, was to be kind until you can't.

"I'm not worried about him," he murmured the lie and looked away from their knowing gazes.

He huddled beneath the blanket.

Worried?

Hell fucking yes, he was worried and not just about facing Dalton, but of Dalton finding out he was Sphinx.

It might all be for nothing because according to Leslie, Dalton never came home for Christmas anymore.

Colton drove up the steep hill and around the first bend. They passed near the orphanage Adam had been placed in after his last foster parents had been arrested for child abuse.

Abuse in the form of they'd taken in one too many kids and used the money for partying instead of food. He and his brother had both been placed in the same home because the foster system tried to do that whenever possible. Only, the system was flawed, or rather, theirs had been. Overworked caseworkers with too many cases and far too many children couldn't make the routine welfare checks. Eventually, they'd caught up with their foster parents when one of the teachers had spoken up about their concern for his wellbeing.

He'd been thirteen and far too small and skinny due to

having missed so many meals. Randy, at seventeen, had taken to stealing food for them to eat. As it always did, his chest hurt thinking of his brother. He sent a silent thank you to the universe that Randy had met Dalton at school the same year they'd been sent to the orphanage.

If not for that friendship, Leslie might not have discovered him scrounging through her trash cans for food while he waited for Randy to come out of the Webers' house.

At that moment in time, he hadn't met any of Dalton's family yet, but he knew the address because Randy had made him memorize it.

The trash cans had been sitting at the curb outside of the gates, so he'd thought what was inside them was free. He'd run from her, but Leslie had been sneaky and had gone back in the house to fetch a sandwich piled high with meat and cheese. She'd left the food on the curb and called out to him before disappearing back inside. He'd darted out of the bushes, grabbed the food, and had eaten it so fast, he'd gotten a stomachache.

"Goofball," Randy had said when his brother had eventually come out of the house. "That's my friend's mom. I'll take you to meet her."

His and Randy's lives had changed forever after that day.

It was the day Leslie had refused to let them go back to the orphanage. She knew some pretty powerful people—all he knew was that a governor had been involved in calling the orphanage.

It was also the day he'd become enamored with Dalton, who enthusiastically showed them to their new, grand bedrooms.

Honestly, he'd fallen in love with Dalton that day watching the joy of giving fill the other boy's eyes.

Call it insta-love, a childish teenage crush, or whatever,

but he'd never reacted to another person like he had with Dalton.

Sometimes, the heart wanted what the heart wanted, even if it wasn't good for you, he reminded himself.

At thirteen, Adam had stood in the bedroom doorway gawking, not at the room but at Dalton, like a lovesick fool.

Both Randy and Dalton had ignored him until Dalton noticed the black eye Adam had been given at school.

"We'll be right back," Dalton had growled, and even at the age of eighteen, the boy was a force.

"Where are your parents, sweetie?" Leslie had pulled him away from the doorway of the bedroom and back down the stairs.

"Dead." Because he wanted the nice-smelling lady to like him, he didn't explain that he and Randy had been taken away from their deadbeat, drug-addicted parents.

"Oh, sweetie," she'd said, pulling him into a hug. Tears had burned his eyes at the unaccustomed tenderness.

"Where are they going?" He'd tossed a glance at the front door.

"Oh, don't worry," Leslie had said, drawing him into a brightly lit kitchen that smelled of rich food and pastries. "Dalton won't beat anyone up. He's too levelheaded for that."

He hadn't been so sure about that, but whatever Randy and Dalton had done that day, he didn't have any more problems from the bully at school from that moment forward.

The only problem he'd had was that he mooned over Dalton and was devastated when the man had joined the Marines after graduating high school.

The vehicle rocked on the road, tugging him back into the warmth of the van. The tires spun, then caught and held as they rounded the bend.

His breath caught as it always had at the sight of the Webers' house. House wasn't the right word to describe the red brick mansion with its manicured lawns piled high with snow. The structure sat behind tall, wrought iron gates. A man at the guardhouse opened the gates and Colton pulled the van through and past a black limousine parked in the circular driveway.

"I've got your room all ready," Mary said, sliding out when the van parked and then helping Renee out of the back. "It's your old one next to mine in the west wing."

He grabbed his backpack and stepped out. The freshly salted sidewalk crackled beneath his feet.

The snow lay in drifts of white around the house and hung on the massive, sloped roofs.

He was still in awe of the place.

"Adam, welcome home, son."

He almost burst into tears at the sound of Dalton's father calling him son. Walking up the steps, he didn't stop until he was inside of the big man's outstretched arms and tightly returning Daniel Weber's hug.

"Come on inside, lunch is ready. I worked all morning on it," Leslie urged them all. While the Weber family employed a cook, Leslie always gave the staff time off during the holidays.

There was no mention that he'd virtually abandoned them thirteen years ago. No mention of him disappearing after Dalton had ended things. What could he say if they asked? *After I joined the service, I was discharged a few years later and vanished into the CIA?*

He hadn't wanted to leave them, but he also hadn't wanted to look back after Dalton had ripped his heart out. Sure, he'd seen Dalton at Randy's funeral, but had any of them ever tried to find him before that? Had Dalton? No.

He took a deep breath and shoved the memories away.

And for the first time in over a decade, he stepped inside of the only place he'd ever called home.

CHAPTER EIGHT

Dalton

IT WAS JUST AFTER MIDNIGHT AND THE JUNKYARD REMAINED EMPTY. Regret soured his stomach and he squeezed his empty coffee cup. Sphinx hadn't responded to his message asking if they were still on, and his silence spoke volumes.

Ace still hadn't heard back from the SecDef, so they were running blind here. He shifted in his spot from inside the junkyard fence. Between the stacks of vehicles, he had what he thought to be the perfect hiding and observation spot. He placed the empty paper cup down on the fender of the vehicle next to him and wondered how much longer he should wait as it was going on midnight.

A piece of metal clanged near the big, dark building that held the junkyard's office and he eased back between the stacks of cars and a nearby pile of junk.

Sphinx wouldn't make a noise like that, and he knew

damned well it wasn't the FBI on his ass since his team had found their fucking bug.

It was probably a rat.

Not taking any chances, he silently drew his Glock from his shoulder holster and slowly moved through the junkyard in the direction of the noise.

Soon enough, he spotted two men—one tall, thin, and longhaired, the other beefy but not with hard muscle, softer and out of shape. He could only see their outlines until they moved back into the light over the closed junkyard office door. So, it was rats, just bigger than he'd expected. What were they doing there? Robbing the place?

"This isn't the place," the longhaired one bitched.

"Yes, it is. This is the only junkyard in town," the beefy one said.

"Then we missed him."

"The boss is going to be pissed."

"Who cares? Let him fucking find Sphinx."

No, not robbers. They were working for someone who wanted Sphinx, and probably dead.

Who was this "boss" they spoke of? When Beefy and Longhair turned away, he skirted around and came at them from the side. Punching the big one in the head, he anticipated Longhair's move when he pulled a weapon. Yanking the beefy one around and in front of him, he blocked Longhair's shot.

The man paused, the gun pointed at them.

"Put your gun down or he's dead," he warned, putting his Glock to the guy's temple.

"If you catch us, we're dead anyway," Longhair said in a flat voice.

Dalton's mind raced, turning over the information.

"That's not true," he urged calmly. "Don't do anything stupid."

"Don't shoot," Beefy begged.

"Tell Sphinx we're sorry," Longhair said, catching him by surprise before he fired his weapon. Beefy guy slumped to the ground.

He shoved away from the big man to avoid getting shot if the bullet went all the way through. Returning fire, he put a slug in Longhair's chest. The man stumbled, falling hard to the ground, and the gun dropped and skidded beneath a car. Longhair's shot had killed Beefy, and Dalton stepped over the body.

Crouching next to Longhair, he put a hand on the man's gasping chest and stared down into his eyes.

"Why do you want me to tell Sphinx you're sorry?"

Longhair gasped, choking on his own blood.

"Who sent you?" he pressed.

"Fe…Fe…"

Dalton leaned down, and with his last dying breath, Longhair whispered, "Feds."

A chill swept down his back. The pair of men were fucking informants? How the fuck did Sphinx know these guys? Had these two told the FBI that Sphinx would be here? How the fuck did they even know about the junkyard? More importantly, where the fuck was Sphinx? Dalton had more questions than ever.

This shit stank.

Boom!

An explosion rocked the junkyard and metal blew apart, shattering the air with fire and smoke. He rolled onto his back and kept on rolling until he was beneath the protection of a pile of demolished cars.

Gunfire echoed in the air, and he shoved to his feet and

ran. Bullets peppered the cars near his body, and he kept on running in the opposite direction from where he'd left his SUV.

Getting out alive was more important. He had no idea how many men they'd sent. Dodging beneath the metal of a smashed delivery truck, he pulled his cell phone out and punched in Ace's number.

"Dalton, how'd it go?"

"It didn't. I'm at the junkyard, under attack. I need a pickup," he said and kept moving. Ducking down another row of junk, he climbed over a pile that looked stable before he jumped off the other side and landed near the fence.

"Fuck, I'm on my way," Ace shouted, keys jangling. He pictured his boss running across the facility room and out the door. "Ten minutes, Dalton. Give me ten fucking minutes. You get the fuck out and disappear. I'll call when I get close."

"On it," he said and closed the phone. He didn't look back; he leaped at the fence and pulled himself up the chain link. At the top, he pulled off his jacket and tossed it over the barbed wire, then slid over the top. He left his jacket and jogged down the dark industrial park's sidewalk. He was a block away when Ace called him back.

"I'm on the corner of South and Jones," he said after glancing at the street signs.

Ace's truck barreled down the street and screeched to a stop. Dalton jumped in and slammed the door and Ace floored it.

"What the fuck happened?" Ace growled, racing around the block and back toward the junkyard entrance.

He explained about the pair of men he suspected were informants. "I think they were there to kill Sphinx and I think the FBI showed up to clean house afterward."

Ace pulled up to the junkyard, right behind a big black

SUV with tinted windows. Agents were milling about looking stupid.

Both he and Ace stepped out of the truck.

"And here's the killer right now," Agent Sweenie said, or maybe that was Swather. No, wait… yeah, it was Sweenie, the guy had puffed up his chest. Swather moved up next to his partner.

"Arrest him," Swather said, pointing a finger at Dalton.

"Fuck you," Dalton growled, clenching his fists. "I'm no killer."

"You shot two men dead. I have an eyewitness that says you killed them in cold blood."

"What eyewitness, you?" He glared at Sweenie.

The man's face turned ugly.

"Shut the fuck up," Ace snapped. "Where's your boss?"

"He's over by the office." Sweenie pointed to the open gate.

"Wait here," Ace ordered him. His boss advanced farther into the junkyard and disappeared from view.

Swather turned toward him with his cuffs out.

"You come near me with those and it will be the last thing your hand ever does," he warned.

The guy stopped and swallowed. It was a long ten minutes filled with distant shouting and then a silent calm descended over the area. After another moment, Ace reappeared.

"Let's go."

He jumped back into his boss's truck and Ace drove them to where he'd parked his SUV.

"How'd that go?"

"I put Farnsworth on the phone with the SecDef."

He laughed. "And?"

"Dave ordered Farnsworth to back off, so we'll see." Ace pulled up and idled next to his SUV.

"I'll meet you back at the office," he said, opening the door.

"I'm headed home, Dalton. It's two o'clock in the morning." Ace frowned at him.

Dalton glanced at his watch. "Oh, yeah."

"Go home," Ace ordered. "Better yet, go home for Christmas."

"Nah. I haven't been back but twice in thirteen years."

"Why's that?"

He thought of big blue eyes and wild curly hair and shrugged. "The stupidity of my youth."

Ace chuckled. "Families forgive."

"I'm not so sure of that."

"Well, whatever you do, the office is closed for two weeks. Get some rest."

"Maybe." He slid from the truck and turned back. "I might see if Sphinx will answer another message."

"All right, man, keep me posted. Have a good night."

He shut the door and stood on the darkened sidewalk watching Ace's truck disappear. Then, sliding behind the wheel of his own SUV, he started it but sat there for a moment and checked his email on his laptop. Maybe Sphinx had responded to the message he'd sent after the fiasco at the apartment. His heartbeat quickened when he found an unread email sent only half an hour earlier.

Sorry, D,

No can do.

I'm unavailable for a few weeks, S.

Well, shit... He closed his laptop and sat for a while.

The emptiness inside his truck seeped into the quiet stillness.

CHAPTER NINE

Adam

H E STRETCHED AND ROLLED OVER ONTO HIS STOMACH AND FOUND his face pressed into mounds of scented softness.

Smiling, he rolled onto his back in the fluffy bedding and flung out his arms and legs on the king-sized bed. Vanilla engulfed him and the pajamas he wore twisted, but he didn't care.

Colton's pajamas were far too big for his frame, but they were warm and smelled like fresh soap. And so did he. He'd taken advantage of the jacuzzi-sized bathtub and had soaked and scrubbed away the filth and grime of the past week.

He'd missed this room, this house, this family.

Dalton, he missed Dalton. His thoughts always wandered back to dangerous territory. It was understandable, though. As a boy, he'd idolized Dalton, always from afar while trying to keep his feelings hidden.

That was until Adam had turned eighteen and then all bets were off, and on Dalton's next leave home from the Marines, he'd gone after Dalton with every bone in his body. At twenty-three years old, it hadn't taken long for Dalton's youthful lust to rise, and they'd met every chance they could. They'd made plans for the future, and Adam had lived for Dalton's leave time and the phone calls. The next few years had passed blissfully.

Until Dalton came home on leave and abruptly ended everything.

Blindsided, Adam had reacted. He had to do something, anything, to make Dalton see him as a man. But when Dalton refused to return any of his texts or phone calls, Adam had joined the Army.

He still cringed thinking of how he'd pleaded, the messages recording how he'd desperately begged for Dalton to love him.

The military had been his move designed to forget about Dalton, and it had worked.

Somewhat.

He rolled to his side with a sigh and blinked at the clock. The bright red numbers showed five after eight in the bright, sunny room. He'd slept over ten hours. More than he'd slept in a long, long time. He felt almost human. Sitting up, he swung his legs over the side of the bed.

A knock sounded on the adjoining door and he called out, "I'm awake."

Mary poked her head through the connecting door and smiled.

"What'd you have, your ear glued to the door?" He lifted one eyebrow.

"Yes! And it's about time! Geez, I thought you were going

to sleep the day away." With that said, Mary ran across the room and jumped on the bed, making him bounce.

He rubbed his hands over his face. "I feel like I could."

"You can nap later! We have a shit ton of stuff to do. Renee is too pregnant to help and Chris is working, so it's you and me."

"Who's Chris again?"

"Renee's husband."

"And Colton can't help because?"

"He and Dad are going to get the trees," she reminded him with an eye roll and leaped back off the bed.

When Mary said trees, she meant plural. The Webers always had a tree in the entryway, one in front of the living room window, and the biggest tree of all would sit in the great room where the family gathered.

"Don't forget about Saturday!"

He groaned. "I don't want to think about it! Besides, it's two days away. Do I need to attend?"

"Yes! Remember, James will be there!" She waggled her eyebrows. "Plus, we need to get you something to wear."

Mary sailed from the room and closed the door without waiting for him to answer.

All he remembered from his childhood about James Cogingsworth was he was ten years older than Adam and James had come to the house often, making it a habit to ask him out. He'd been dating Dalton and hadn't had eyes for anyone else. Adam had always said no and laughed it off, but James assured him he'd wait.

Adam plopped back on the bed. It didn't matter, James could wait the rest of his life, Adam wasn't interested. Mary had told him that James had inherited his daddy's fortune. A billionaire! Mary had clapped her hands. It didn't matter.

The last thing he was looking for was another complication in his life.

He gave up trying to go back to sleep and slid from the bed. Glancing around for his backpack, it came up missing. That was when he noticed the pile of clothes with a note sitting on the Victorian-style chair near an antique desk. He picked up the note.

All washed! Love, Mom.

He blinked back the burning of his eyes. Fuck, he was an elite operative, a former CIA agent, with no time for tears. But he was also human, and in the face of the Weber family's love, he was pudding.

He jumped into a shower stall that could fit five people easily and was washed, dressed, and heading out of his room twenty minutes later while finger combing his hair. Mary's bedroom door was open and when he poked his head inside, he found it empty.

Walking down the paisley, cream-colored carpeted hallway, he paused to gaze at the large family portraits along the way. The newest photo of the Webers was missing Dalton in it.

He kept walking until he found the one he wanted. One of the ones where he and Randy had been included. God, he'd been young; he looked like a fucking baby, smiling at the camera as if nothing on earth could kill his joy.

In the picture, Dalton had already gotten a few tattoos, but now he had a ton more from what Adam had seen in the shadowy light of the apartment complex. He studied Dalton's face and mentally compared it to the one from the other night. The man was still hands-down sexy as hell.

"There you are." Mary came to stand beside him and gazed up at the portrait. "That's the last one we have with us all together."

"Yeah," he said over the lump in his throat.

"Oh, Adam. I'm so sorry. My brother is an idiot," Mary said and linked her arm with his and popped a kiss on his cheek.

"No. He was young. Too young to know what he wanted." Or maybe Dalton just hadn't wanted him. He shook off the irritating thought. "We were both too young to talk about forever."

"That's not true," Mary argued. "Mom and Dad met and married at eighteen and twenty. Love does happen that fast."

Fast? Were two years together as a couple fast? Probably. At eighteen, everything felt exaggerated. As a man, he could honestly look back on him and Dalton and know they probably wouldn't have made it. Thinking they were meant to be forever had been a childish dream on his part.

He drew in a breath and turned away from the photo. "What about you? Anyone new in your life?"

"I'm dating a nice young man who will be here for Christmas."

"What's his name, where does he live, and I need his occupation." He frowned.

She rolled her eyes with a laugh and pulled him down the hallway. "Oh, hell no. I know how you military men are! Dalton came home and tried to chase my last one away."

"When was this?" he asked, laughing.

"Just after you joined the Army."

"What?" He stopped walking and pulled her around.

"What?" she said.

"Dalton came home?"

"Yes." She looked confused.

"When exactly was this?"

"He came back a month later after your…" She swallowed. "After your breakup."

"He did?" he asked stupidly as if this wasn't Dalton's home and he couldn't come back anytime he wished. But if Dalton came back a month after their breakup, that meant Dalton had taken another military leave to do so. That was weird.

"It doesn't matter, he's only been home one time since then." She tugged on him, but he refused to budge.

Dalton had come back after breaking up with him? He couldn't get over that fact. So that probably meant Dalton had kept tabs on him in the military. Had Dalton been able to find out that he'd later joined the CIA? Probably not.

"Wait…Dalton has only been home two times in the past decade?" he gaped at Mary, his feet coming to a standstill.

"Thirteen years, but yeah. Once that month after your breakup. That's when he found out you'd enlisted," she said.

"And the other time?"

She looked away. "He flew home after Randy's funeral and stayed for three days. Hardly said a word the whole time. He hasn't been back since."

Well, fuck him stupid. He started walking again. "He won't come home this time, will he?" He glanced around as they descended the wide staircase that separated the four levels of the mansion.

"Nope, trust me. He won't come home."

The softly spoken words made his chest ache and he rubbed the spot through his shirt as they reached the bottom of the stairs.

Sugary baking dough and spices drifted in the air and he could hear the soft sound of "Jingle Bells" piped in through the overhead speakers.

"She made pastries." He said in awe and his mouth watered.

"She made pastries. Plus, there's left over cake from last

night," Mary echoed with a giggle and shoved him through the kitchen door.

They'd surprised him last night with a cake after dinner to belatedly celebrate his birthday and he'd spent a good portion of the time blinking back the sting in his eyes.

Inside the large, bright room, the center table that could fit the Knights of the Round Table was filled with every one of his favorite breakfast foods—from bacon, eggs, hash browns, and chocolate chip pancakes to piping hot cinnamon rolls.

He was glad that the growl his stomach made was drowned out by the music.

"Good morning, lovely." Leslie rushed over and hugged him tightly and then fingered one of his wild curls. "Hungry?"

"Starving."

Everyone in the room laughed and Leslie urged him into a chair next to Mary. The room broke out with noisy conversations as dishes were served.

He ate and smiled so much his cheeks hurt.

"I'm so glad you called Mom," Mary whispered to him.

God, so was he... so was he.

He hugged her tightly and she stole a piece of his bacon.

They laughed uncontrollably, and it was the sort of laughter when you only had to look at a person to keep laughing.

It felt like heaven.

CHAPTER TEN

Dalton

Two days later, he was pulled from a sound sleep by birds fighting right outside of his window.

Not even rolling over, he tossed his spare pillow at the window. It fell short. Yeah, like that was going to shut them up.

Damn it, Ace. He hated vacations. It gave him too much time to think.

The man had forced him to take time off, and while Dalton had still gone into the office a few hours each day, for the most part, he'd tried to rest.

Rolling over in his bed, he blinked up at the light creeping across the ceiling. A strange loneliness lingered and on impulse, he snagged his cell phone from the nightstand.

As always, he pulled up Adam's number and stared at it. How many times had he called and hung up without saying a word? Only a handful of times. *Fucking stalker*. He rubbed a hand down his face. Six years since he'd seen Adam face to face, but it had been thirteen since Dalton had last held him. So sue him if he made a few calls just to hear his voice.

Scrolling past Adam's number, he punched a finger at his sister's name. Thankfully, she answered on the first ring.

"Hey chickee," he teased.

"Dalton!" his sister squeaked.

"Mary!" he mimicked like they'd done as kids.

"Hey, big bro, how the hell are you?"

"Oh, you know, busy, busy." He smiled at nothing, gazing at the ceiling fan over his bed and waited. This was the part where she forced him to talk to their mother so his mom could turn the guilt screws about not coming home for Christmas.

"I know, I know," she continued on a laugh, and he heard a door shut.

"What do you know?" he grinned.

"You're not coming home again!" she sang. "It's okay, I'll pass your regrets on to Mom," she finished with a promise and then launched into baby shower stuff and off the topic of Christmas completely.

Well, that was damned odd.

"So…" He interrupted her chatter five minutes later. "Are you dreading the big Christmas celebration?" he probed.

He waited with a smile. His sister typically bitched about having to decorate the massive ballroom herself—which she didn't really do herself because they hired people for that—but Mary loved to dig the knife of guilt into him.

"What? No! You know, it's going to be small and all," she rushed out.

Okay… something was definitely off. His family never

did the holidays small, *ever*. Every year around this time, his parents put on a community ball.

For. The. Whole. Community.

Small my ass. He frowned. Why was Mary lying to him? His brain flew through different possibilities, and he latched on to one he couldn't shake. One that made his chest sink. Maybe Mary wasn't lying.

"Is someone ill?"

"What? No!" She laughed. "The only one ill is Renee on account she's pregnant again."

"Yeah, I know that," he said impatiently.

"Anywho," Mary said. "I've got to run. Love you, bro."

"Love you too." He barely got the words out before she hung up.

The sun peaked through the blinds and hit his pillow and he moved his head. After another moment of lying there, he plucked his phone up again and checked his email. Surely there would be messages from his family? They always started an email chain around this time of year. There were none. His email was strangely quiet for it being almost Christmas.

Scrolling through his call log, he stared at the screen and hovered his finger over his mother's cell phone number. Maybe they were having financial problems? No, that couldn't be right. The whole family lived under the same roof and helped support the estate. Not to mention, his father came from old money and his mother was a popular romance author whose books sold internationally.

He hadn't been back to Alaska since he'd flown there right after Randy's funeral. He'd only done so because it was the only place he'd felt close to Adam. And he'd needed that after his first glimpse of a fully matured Adam Campbell.

Squeezing the phone, he cradled it to his chest and punched his mom's number.

It rang.

She always picked up, and he took a breath to issue a cheery good morning.

The phone rang again.

And then again, before it went to voicemail.

He hung up with a lump in his throat. He couldn't ever remember a time that his mother hadn't picked up. Perhaps Mary had shared that they talked? It didn't matter, his mom always picked up the phone.

Fuck this. He rolled from his bed and gazed around at his studio apartment. He owned it, but was rarely in the small space. That he was there now grated on his nerves. He pulled up the Delta airlines app on his cell and booked the seat the airline kept reserved under the Weber family name.

He didn't feel guilty one bit.

Since his family liked to keep secrets by avoiding him, he'd show up unannounced. With his decision made, he showered, packed, and ordered an Uber. He sent a text to Ace letting him know he was heading to Alaska after all.

• • •

On his second lengthy layover, he realized he wouldn't be able to get a car this late at night. Plus, he couldn't call the limo from the house because two back-to-back storms were heading right through Fairbanks.

Forgoing the surprise of his visit, he sent a text to his brother.

Flying Delta home. Landing at 10:45 PM. Pick me up.

By the time the airline called boarding for his last connecting flight, Colton still hadn't returned his call. He slid into a seat normally reserved for airline executives—one of which was his cousin—and stretched out his legs. He rarely took advantage of the perk, but since his cousin wasn't coming home for Christmas and Dalton was desperate, it worked out.

"Can I get you anything, Mr. Weber?" the flight attendant gushed.

He smiled. "Coffee, please."

She hurried off and his phone finally pinged with a message from his brother.

Sure, I'll be there.

It was short and sweet. The odd part was that Colton usually called him whenever he sent a text because they rarely if ever talked. What the hell was going on? A few more hours and he'd have his answers. His younger, kindhearted brother always shared with him.

The flight went smoothly, if a bit rocky on the landing, and he stalked through the airport and out into the bitter cold. He pulled his new coat tight as he stepped into the chilly air. His other jacket still hung over the barbed wire fence at the junkyard.

It was hard to miss the huge Jeep with the name *Weber* on the side and he tossed his bag in the backseat before sliding into the passenger seat.

"Hey, bro," Colton said, pulling away from the curb once Dalton had shut the door and buckled up.

"Hey." He turned sideways in his seat to gaze at his brother, but Colton kept his eyes on the road. "What the hell is going on?"

"What?" Colton tossed him a frown.

"Not you too." He squinted at his younger brother. "Mary was acting all weird."

"How?"

"She didn't beg me to come home."

Colton sent him a hard look that sort of took him aback. "Maybe she's tired of asking. Maybe we all are."

Were they? Is that what this was all about? He'd stayed away so long that they no longer wanted him here? Or had he stayed away so long that they never expected him to come home?

"I've been busy." He turned to face the road.

Outside, flurries hit the windshield, but they were so light, they melted away quickly. Colton took the turnoff and drove up the incline that would eventually lead them to the house.

"Busy? It's been years." Colton's voice was hard. "We've all been busy, but we've managed to come home for the holidays."

The guilt ate at him and he rubbed at the heartburn starting in his sternum. Colton made him feel like an asshole. Hell, he was an asshole.

"You fucking live here," he reminded his brother.

"You know what I meant," Colton snapped back.

"I had my reasons."

"What reasons? That we took Adam's side in the breakup? Is that what caused you to disown your family?" Colton said flatly.

Disown? He stared in shock. Where the hell had that come from? Sure, at first, he'd been pissed that they'd sided with Adam, but after a while, he'd gotten over it. He'd stayed the fuck away because every inch of that mansion reminded him of Adam.

His throat grew tight and he gazed at his little brother, wondering where the easygoing man had gone. They used to be best friends, buddies who shared everything. Now, Colton was like a stranger. Or maybe it was him who was the stranger.

"You were in the wrong," Colton continued. "Dead wrong, and you caused Adam to run away."

He clenched his teeth. "He ended up okay."

"By joining the Army?" Colton snorted.

Dalton gave an annoyed sigh and turned to gaze out the window.

The dark tossed his own reflection back at him.

"Besides, you knew you were in the wrong," his brother went on. "That's why you took additional leave and came back a month later."

"I came back to make sure he was okay."

And to make sure the rumor of Adam joining the military was a lie, but he'd been too late. He would have called, but Adam had changed his number. *That was because you cut him off.* He rubbed at his chest.

"Sure, keep telling yourself that," Colton drawled, easing the Jeep up and around another bend. "I've always been curious. Why the hell did you run home after Randy's funeral?"

He stiffened at the accusing tone in Colton's voice. "I didn't *run* home, I came to visit. Besides, what I do is none of your business!" He crossed his arms and then uncrossed them to clench his fists on his thighs.

"It was Randy's funeral. Don't you think Adam might have wanted to talk to you? Did you even say anything to him?"

Where the hell was Colton getting his information from? He scowled at his brother.

"I did say something!"

"What? Sorry for your loss?" Colton growled.

He swallowed. "I was sorry."

So fucking sorry. More than he could say. He'd lost touch with Randy, and he'd let fear drive him apart from the only person on earth he'd ever truly—

"You're an asshole." Colton broke through his thoughts, yanking him back from the gaping hole of memories.

"You don't know the whole story," he growled.

"Story?"

He held his brother's gaze and held his tongue. Adam's marital status wasn't his fucking story to tell.

Colton squinted at him for a long moment. "Maybe I don't know the whole story, but you're still an asshole."

"So they say." He looked out the window and could just make out the lights of the orphanage in the distance. Bright blue eyes and curly dark hair swam in his vision. The silence was only broken by the tires crunching on crusted snow.

When they reached the mansion, Colton pulled over to the side of the road rather than driving through the gates the guard had opened.

"What now?" He turned on Colton. Hadn't he suffered enough of his brother's judgmental wrath?

Colton squeezed the wheel and let out a sigh before turning to look at him.

"He's here."

"What?" Dalton frowned, the words not computing. "Who's here?"

"Adam."

His world shifted. The Jeep suddenly seemed too small and his airway closed.

"For once in your life, think about someone other than yourself," Colton growled over the rushing in his ears and put the Jeep in drive.

Dalton gripped the *oh-shit* handle over the door and hung on like it was a fucking lifeline.

Adam. Oh fuck, Adam was here?

Like a dream come true or a nightmare depending on which way he looked at it. Was the fiancé here too? Or was the guy Adam's husband now?

Colton guided the vehicle through the numerous cars lining the driveway and parked it at the front steps.

A footman stepped up to the Jeep doors, but waited.

"I didn't tell the family I was picking you up. They don't know you're home. I left a tux in your room."

"Tux?" It was all he could latch on to.

"The ball has already started."

He snapped his head to the door and found people wandering up the wide steps and into the mansion in all forms of dresses, suits, and tuxes.

After that shocking bit of news, Colton left him and disappeared into the crowd.

It took him a good few moments to work up the nerve to follow.

"Welcome home, sir," the footman said, holding his door open.

Welcome? Was he? He murmured a thank you and slowly followed the crowd of people into his home.

CHAPTER ELEVEN

Adam

He spun in James' arms to the music piped in over their heads and smiled.

He could do normal. As a master of disguise, he could blend in and act the perfect house guest. It came with his training. Only, this house wasn't just any house, it had been his home, and acting happy and normal took extra finesse.

The slow waltz ended and he gave a small bow to James.

"Call me?" James caught his hand before he could walk away.

"Sure," he smoothly lied with another smile, having no intention of calling James, ever.

Adam made his way over to where the Webers had gathered at one of the lavishly decorated tables. White draping tablecloths fell to the floor over each round surface and gold, green, and red holiday decorations were displayed on the top of the sixty tables. A place setting to the right of Mary held a small sign that simply read, *Adam*.

"So?" Mary hissed when he slipped into his seat.

"No." He shot her a stern look.

"Not the one? Ok, well there's Thomas over there, he's from really old money. Way older than James' billions."

"And way older than James too," he snorted, not even looking at the man who was old enough to be his grandfather. "Thomas is married. Now knock it off."

"What, her? I heard they're getting divorced. Wait... You're not taken, are you?" Mary asked out of the blue, eyeing him suspiciously.

He glanced away and she grabbed at his hand, gripping it hard. "Are you?"

"No, not any longer."

Music, laughter, and the hum of conversation drifted through the room. Cinnamon and cloves filled the air and the lights on the large tree at the end of the room twinkled. It really was beautiful. They'd done a good job on the decorations.

"But you were?" Mary whispered and he finally turned back to hold her gaze.

"Six years ago, I was engaged."

Her pretty mouth turned down. "What happened?"

Your brother happened, he wanted to say, but he kept the words locked away.

"It didn't work out."

"That usually means it was money, job, or someone cheated."

He frowned and tugged his hand away. "It does not. We just decided it wasn't going to work." To be fair, he'd decided to end it, and while Michael had been furious, the man had honored his wishes.

"Liar."

He rolled his eyes. "How would you know?"

"Because you have been, and always will be, in love with my brother." Her smile was smug.

"Where the hell did that come from?" He gaped at her.

"Admit it."

"You're wrong, I am not," he said firmly. "What Dalton and I had was…"

"Love," she insisted.

"We were kids," he murmured, running his gaze over the crowded room. People were milling about. Either dancing, eating, or in groups jockeying around a fully stocked bar.

"You just told me you broke up with your fiancé six years ago…" She tapped a pretty pink nail against her lips. "That was around the time of Randy's funeral, wasn't it?"

He knew by the look in her eyes that she'd put two and two together. Let her have her pipe dream of him and Dalton. It wouldn't come true, so what was the harm?

He pressed his lips tightly together and turned away from the knowing look in her pretty eyes to roam his gaze over the crowded room.

His eyes landed on a man near the entrance.

The air left his lungs and the room closed in. He struggled to draw in a breath and when he did, it came out as a gasp.

Wide shoulders filled the space around the guy and dark hair fell to just above the man's collar. The lights overhead reflected on onyx-colored hair. The cut of the tux molded tightly over his shoulders, arms, and hips. Lifting a hand, the guy rubbed at his nape, appearing uncomfortable as fuck.

Adam's eyes became mesmerized by the rubbing hand.

Fingers with tattoos. He was a sucker for a guy with muscles and ink…

Oh fuck.

He grew lightheaded waiting for Dalton to turn around.

"Oh, for shit's sake," Mary hissed.

"What?" he choked out, dragging his gaze from Dalton.

"Don't freak out." She clutched his hand hard.

Too late.

"About what?" he murmured.

"It's Dalton. He's home."

The blood had already left his face. His stomach churned and he swung his gaze back to Dalton.

This time, Dalton was looking right back at him. Straight into his eyes and right into his fucking soul.

Those eyes, those fucking gold-colored eyes, like the warmth of whiskey. He couldn't see the color from across the distance, but he knew that shade as surely as he knew his own.

He also knew he'd never forget how cruel Dalton could be.

He stood in a rush and Mary caught his chair before it could topple over and make a scene. Turning in the opposite direction, he walked quickly toward one of the side doors.

Call him a coward.

So the fuck what? He was.

Not only was he not ready to face Dalton, but the man also had no clue who he really was. Or did he? No! But there was a very good chance that Dalton would recognize him as Sphinx if he got close enough. Even though he'd been covered from head to toe in black, Dalton was scary observant. Yeah, Dalton had the uncanny ability to notice the unnoticeable.

Shoving through the patio doors, he reached the outside

and sucked in huge gulps of the cold Alaskan air. He hurried down the salted walkway that ran along the side of the house until he reached the south entrance rear door. Every inch of the mansion was etched into his brain; once back inside, he'd be able to lose anyone in seconds.

Stepping through the entrance, he let out the breath he was holding and closed the door.

A throat cleared.

His feet froze on the linoleum floor and he snapped his gaze around before he found him. How the fuck had Dalton known what entrance he'd use? The answer to that question, and any words for that matter, seemed to have deserted him.

Dalton took a step forward and Adam held his ground. No way in hell would he let Dalton intimidate him.

No fucking way. He narrowed his eyes and flattened his lips, and his look stopped Dalton cold in his tracks.

Yet, a curious light filled the man's eyes.

Shit. With his silent challenge, he'd piqued Dalton's curiosity. It was the last thing he wanted.

Cold eyes and flat lips were not the Adam of old, and by the look on Dalton's face, he had noticed.

Well, he had news for Dalton Weber—he was no longer that Adam. He wasn't the Adam from his youth and he damned well wasn't the Adam that Dalton had met at Randy's funeral. He'd changed since that time. He'd become harder since ending things with Michael.

He took assignments that made grown men's balls shrivel. Dalton had no idea what he was capable of.

He ran his eyes over the ink running down the sides of Dalton's neck before disappearing beneath his collar. A small silver hoop in Dalton's left earlobe matched the rings on his fingers.

The fucking ass hadn't said a word, but then that was

Dalton. Always waiting until Adam lost his cool and asked why the fuck he wasn't talking.

Well, he wasn't talking first this time. He'd talked at the funeral, asking Dalton to stay, but other than leaving Adam with harshly whispered words of condolences, Dalton couldn't be bothered.

"I'll be out come morning," he said through his teeth and then clenched his fists. Fuck, shit, damn it.

The sexy smile toying at the edge of Dalton's mouth disappeared in a flash.

"Don't leave." The deep, sleepy-sounding rumble drifted between them, reaching into his chest like fucking tendrils of... of... of he didn't know what, but it pissed him off.

"I don't want to be here when you're here."

"I'm sorry."

"What?"

"You heard me."

He squinted, holding those warm golden eyes, eyes he could now clearly see. No subterfuge filled their depths, but maybe Dalton had become a really good liar.

"What exactly are you apologizing for?"

Dalton took a step forward and Adam took a step back before he could stop himself.

Dalton stopped abruptly.

Clenching his teeth, Adam tipped his chin and stiffened his spine. He could wipe the floor with this asshole. Surely, Dalton knew he wasn't a pushover, the military had knocked the softness right out of him. *How the hell could Dalton know that?*

Adam squinted and stayed still. He wouldn't tip his hand until he had an escape route worked out. It was December in Alaska for fuck's sake. One couldn't just walk out in the middle of the night.

"All of it."

"What?" It took a moment to regain his train of thought. Oh yeah… Dalton's apology.

"You heard me."

He was pretty sure Dalton had moved closer while he'd been contemplating an escape in his head.

"All of it?" What exactly did that mean?

"All, from when I walked out on you thirteen years ago to walking away at Randy's funeral."

"Fuck you," Adam snapped. "You don't get to say you're sorry after thirteen years and expect to be forgiven."

"I don't expect you to forgive me." Dalton's throat moved in a hard swallow. "It's the truth."

"What do you want?" He squinted. He didn't trust the fucker.

"I don't want you to leave."

"Give me a reason to stay." What the hell? Where the hell had that come from? Fuck, shit, damn it.

Dalton took another step forward.

"Not that!" he snarled, his hands clenched, ready to knock Dalton out if he dared touch him.

Dalton must have sensed his desire to clock him and stopped moving altogether.

"Sorry," Dalton muttered and rubbed at the back of his neck. The guy had a propensity to do that when he was nervous.

Adam glanced at his watch. "I'm waiting."

"Cocky little shit," Dalton growled and took several steps forward.

He may be little, but he'd taken down bigger men than Dalton.

"Go fuck yourself," he snapped.

Dalton lunged, a big hand swiping at him, probably trying to grab his tux or arm, he wasn't sure.

Adam went low.

He dropped and swept his legs out and removed Dalton's legs from beneath him. Dalton crashed to the carpet and Adam leaped over the sprawling form. In midair, his ankle was caught, a hand fisted in his pant leg, and he flew forward. He waited for impact. Only, strong arms caught him around the waist and kept him from falling. Dalton had moved so fucking fast, it took a moment to register. Adam spun and delivered a blow that only became a glancing hit instead of his knee to Dalton's junk.

The big Marine grunted and stumbled but hung on. They crashed into the wall and family photos of vacation trips rattled in their frames.

He cleaved his fingers through Dalton's hair and had only a moment to suck in air before his mouth was taken in a brutal kiss. Adam's fingers fisted dark strands as the kiss grew ferocious and his teeth bit at Dalton's lips, drawing blood. The kiss deepened, grew sluggish and slow, and Dalton moaned.

Adam lifted his legs to wrap around Dalton's waist.

Fuck. Shit. Damn it.

CHAPTER TWELVE

Dalton

ADAM'S TASTE FILLED HIS MOUTH, HEAD, AND FOGGED UP HIS brain.

Like a fucking dream come true.

Those sleek legs wrapped around his waist as he clamped his palms over Adam's ass, squeezing tight.

Memories came rushing up and heat roared through Dalton's gut.

Groaning when fisted hands tightened in his hair, Dalton tightened his grip when Adam's legs lowered and his feet touched the floor. This right here was all he'd ever wanted. He caught Adam's waist harder, but Adam pulled away.

Dalton clenched his teeth and the air left his lungs as he steeled himself for Adam to walk away. A sound left his throat when Adam did the unexpected by gripping the front of his tux and pulling him toward a linen closet.

Dalton went because he couldn't tolerate any distance between them. He wanted Adam, had always wanted him, would forever want him.

The dim light came on from a bulb at the back of the fully stocked room. Adam slammed the door and shoved him back against the wall, into the shadows of the large linen closet. In another second, Adam was back in his arms, biting at his lips and yanking at the opening of his pants. When his cock was freed, Adam sank to his knees and engulfed him in the wet warmth of his mouth.

"Jesus, Cupcake," he growled the nickname he'd given Adam when they were younger and sank his hands in dark curls.

Adam gripped his ass and deep-throated his cock simultaneously. Dalton gasped and slammed one hand to the wall for balance while keeping a hold on the back of Adam's head with the other. His brain exploded; all he could think, feel, and do was fuck that sweet mouth, and crave. God he fucking craved Adam like nothing on earth.

His spine tingled and his balls grew tight.

"Gonna come," he warned as his orgasm rolled over him. Adam mumbled something that sounded like an agreement around his cock. When Adam's hand slipped up his stomach and trailed upward over his chest, he exploded, emptying his balls. Adam sucked and swallowed until he was spent and then sat back on his heels. Dalton's cock hung wetly between them, still semi-hard in the dim lighting of the room.

Adam shoved to his feet, wiping his mouth with a clean towel from one of the folded piles.

Dalton panted. What a homecoming. He reached for Adam, but the man dodged out of the way before flipping on the light. The small bulb sent light through the closet.

Eyeing Adam, Dalton tucked his cock away.

What the hell had just happened?

What did it mean?

None of those questions seemed to fit the situation he found himself in, so he went with a question that made him inwardly cringe.

"Where's the fiancé?" His voice sounded like he'd swallowed rocks.

The tip of Adam's head before he spoke was as familiar to Dalton as his own breathing.

"We broke up." Adam crossed his arms and leaned a shoulder against one of the metal shelves.

"When? Why?" He squinted, trying to read Adam's expression.

"Don't you think we should discuss…" Adam waved a hand at his crotch. "It seems more pertinent."

He honestly didn't know what to say. Was this Adam's way of saying he wanted him back?

"Okay, talk."

Adam's full lips pressed tight. "You talk first."

Dalton took a breath and rubbed at the knot forming at the back of his neck. Okay, he'd go first, but he was starting back a ways, a long ways.

"I tried to call you."

"When?" Adam squinted at him. "After Randy's funeral?"

"Yes, a hundred times but couldn't get up the nerve, but I'm talking about earlier."

The silence stretched. "How much earlier?"

"A few weeks after we broke up." Dalton cleared his throat, referencing what had happened thirteen years ago.

"*We* broke up?" Adam snorted on a derisive sounding laugh. "Let's be real here, you broke up with me. It wasn't a mutual decision."

"I fucked up."

"You sure did," Adam snapped.

"You turned off your phone," Dalton said gruffly.

Adam shrugged. "I got a new number. I figured since you were ignoring all of my texts and phone calls anyway, I'd start fresh with a new one when I joined the Army." The man's mouth curled and his head tipped, dark curls falling forward, and he ached to brush them back.

"I followed your career," Dalton continued, fisting his hands to keep them still.

"Did you?"

One of Adam's eyebrows arched over a skeptical gaze. Eyes that resembled blue fire stared at him through slitted lids.

"Yeah, but I lost track of you after you left the military."

"I was busy." Adam shrugged.

"With?"

"None of your business." Adam pointed to the door, a door he was blocking to prevent Adam from escaping. "Move."

"Don't you want to talk about this?" It was his turn to wave a hand between them.

"Don't think anything into that blow job. That was scratching an itch."

"I thought you said it was pertinent?"

"I lied."

"You know damned well that was more than a blow job," he growled, locking his eyes on Adam's mouth.

"Was it?" The man's lips twitched.

"You want me."

"No, I don't. Don't misunderstand that—" Adam again waved a hand at his crotch, "—as anything other than to get you out of my system."

Awareness sizzled and he knew it wasn't only his own

attraction. Adam wanted him. He could see it in the way the man's throat moved when he swallowed, the way his hands fluttered in the air between them and his eyes darted away. The bulge in the man's pants was hard to miss.

"Let me see your phone," he said.

"What?" A furrow creased across Adam's brow.

"Adam!" Mary's voice drifted down the hall.

"Your phone." Dalton held out his hand.

"She's coming, you better move."

He stayed where he was. "Then you better hurry."

With an exaggerated sigh that made Dalton smile, Adam slapped a cell phone in his hand.

Dalton held the phone to Adam's face and it popped open. Adam's lips pressed into a flat line. He ignored Adam and put his phone number into Adam's cell.

"You changed your number," Dalton said, glancing up from the phone. It wasn't a question.

Adam's frown increased. "How would you know I changed my number?"

"Meet me later. We need to talk."

Adam snatched the phone from him and tucked it away. "Move."

"Say you'll meet me and I'll move," Dalton urged.

"Adam." Mary's voice sounded closer.

"Damn it," Adam hissed. "Okay, I'll meet you!"

"The south terrace off of the breakfast room at two." He glanced at his watch; it was just after midnight. The guests should be gone by then.

Adam glared at him and snatched up a stack of hand towels. Dalton moved when Adam stalked closer, but he didn't make it easy for him. Adam was forced to brush against him on the way out of the room. When the door snapped shut and the light flipped off, he heard his sister's voice right outside the door.

"There you are!"

"Yeah, ran out of clean hand towels in one of the guest bathrooms."

"We have staff for that, silly."

"You know how I feel about that."

Their voices faded and Dalton stood with a stupid smile on his face. Adam hated having people wait on him, and it was nice to know the man's core values hadn't changed. Dalton rubbed at his cock through his pants; remembering Adam's mouth kept him semi-hard.

His cell phone buzzed and he tugged it out, frowning at Ace's number.

"Boss?"

"The SecDef called, and nobody seems to have a copy of the list." Ace's tired sigh came over the phone.

"What do you mean? Does the list even exist?"

"I don't know," Ace responded.

What happened to Sphinx selling a list to the highest bidder? Without that list, there was no case against Sphinx. Something tight released in his chest.

"What the hell is going on?" He frowned, staring at nothing. "Why exactly was Sphinx blacklisted?"

"I don't know." Ace hesitated. "But I need you to meet Farnsworth."

"I'm in fucking Alaska."

"So is he."

He frowned. "What's he doing here?"

"Following Sphinx."

What the fuck was Sphinx doing in Alaska?

CHAPTER THIRTEEN

Adam

He had loved Dalton with every fiber of his being.

And he would have done anything to keep the man, but Dalton hadn't wanted him. The memory of their last day together, when Dalton had broken it off, rose up and a lump grew in his throat.

"I can't see you anymore."

"What? Why?" His heart had pounded so hard, he'd thought he was going to pass out.

"I'm not coming home for a few years. I've reenlisted." Dalton said.

"Reenlisted?" He'd sounded stupid. "I thought you were discharging…you said we'd buy a house."

He cringed remembering how his voice had wobbled. There'd been no house, and Dalton had stayed in the Marines for several more years. Adam had never gotten an explanation. Dalton had walked out of that same closet and never looked back. In fact, the breakup had occurred in the same closet, only Dalton had been the one on his knees back then.

It seemed fitting that he had returned the favor and gave Dalton head before walking away.

Right?

A little before 2 AM, he sat on the edge of his bed, gazing at the door he'd closed and locked. Not that he thought Dalton would attempt to enter, but he needed privacy to get his shit together.

You gave him a blowjob.

Jesus, he berated himself. He rubbed at his mouth and jumped up and headed to the shower.

As if the warm water could wash away the memory of Dalton. The man's taste had overridden the past and the shallowness of Dalton's coldness in the face of his burning love.

He'd told Mary that their love wouldn't have lasted, but in his heart, he hadn't believed it. He still loved Dalton as strongly as the day he'd first met him, but it didn't matter. This time, he was going to be the one to walk away.

Dalton apologized, that sneaky voice that always took Dalton's side whispered. So what? His pride wasn't going to let him breakdown and seek out Dalton. While the words of sorrow Dalton had muttered sounded sincere, it was too little too late.

Dalton had left him.

He came back.

Much too late!

Too late for them. Their time had passed.

His cock swelled beneath the warm water. It damn well remembered how they'd burned up the sheets. Gnashing his teeth, he snapped off the faucet.

Snatching up a towel, he dried and pulled on a pair of sweatpants.

When his cell phone buzzed, he absently answered it, rubbing the towel over his still damp hair.

"The junkyard where you were to meet Pegasus was hit," his handler said.

"How the hell did they know where I was meeting them?" He sank to the edge of the bed.

"I'm working on it," Richard Black said with a sigh. "I need a quick favor."

"I'm at a party, on holiday."

"It's in your neck of the woods. It shouldn't take long," Black responded.

"You found me in Alaska?"

"Your alias was flagged."

His heart lurched and he sat up straight. "Do they know my location?"

"No, I squashed the alert," Black soothed.

He sighed and dropped back on his bed to stare up at the intricate designs on the ceiling, where gold and white swirls surrounded old-fashioned cherubs and lavishly dressed Egyptians.

"Sphinx?"

What? Now after weeks of feeling like a criminal, his handler wanted him to do a job? Screw that. Plus, he needed to decide if he was going to meet Dalton or disappear.

"Come on, I need you on this."

He rubbed at the knot forming in the back of his neck. "What is it?"

"I have an informant I need you to meet. Just pick up a file and drop it at a locker."

"Location?"

He filed away the location without writing it down. "What's in the file?"

"Need to know."

His lips pressed tightly together. And he didn't need to know? That was one of the problems he had with the agency. Their desire to have him do things without question or without knowing what the fuck was going on.

It was one of the reasons he was in this mess. He'd had a file to deliver and he'd looked at its contents. What a clusterfuck mistake that had been.

The screwed-up part was that Black had been on vacation and Adam had done a job for another handler. Someone named Jones. The dark, robotic voice had requested Adam's assistance. Adam couldn't even tell Black who the fuck Jones was.

Black said there was no log of anyone calling him for a job on that particular day. The log only shows his badge accessing a secure area and taking the file.

Of course, it fucking showed he took it! Adam had been there and he'd taken the file, just as he had been ordered to do.

The only thing he hadn't done was deliver the file to the final destination. Where the fuck the FBI had gotten the idea that he had a list of names was beyond him.

"Have you talked to Scott about meeting me?"

"He's on holiday," Black responded with a sigh.

"That's a long fucking holiday," Adam snapped. "Call him or I'm taking the file to DC." Maybe someone in Washington could take it off his hands.

"Just give me the damned thing and I'll take care of it."

"I told you, I don't want you involved."

"You should have dropped the fucking thing when you

were supposed to and you wouldn't be in this mess," Black growled.

"I couldn't."

Black's irritated-sounding sigh came over the phone.

"And I'm quitting," Adam added, changing the subject.

"Where's that coming from?" Black's voice grew sharper. "I'm working on clearing your name."

"I know, I'm still going to quit after this is over. I want to do something else."

"You're not cut out for anything else."

"How the fuck would you know?"

"I know you, Sphinx."

"Maybe, but I'm still quitting."

"Do this for me and we'll discuss your quitting after your name is clear."

"I supposed tonight's job isn't sanctioned?" he waited, knowing the answer.

"No. I can't offer you sanction when you're blacklisted."

Great. Out in the fucking cold and they ask this of him? Bold fuckers.

"It would be a good time to give me the file," Black said again.

"I'll text when I'm done." He hung up before his handler could respond and before he could lose his temper.

He wasn't giving the video file to anyone without the power to do something.

Once he was dressed in all black, he left the house again only this time, he walked along the row of cars parked in the makeshift lot off to the side of the house.

"Where are you going?"

He whirled around. "Son of a b…!" he bit out, cutting off the last word.

Dalton laughed.

CHAPTER FOURTEEN

Dalton

HE LAUGHED WHEN ADAM JUMPED A MILE HIGH.

"Sorry?"

Slapping one hand on the top of the car, Adam glared at him.

"I have an errand to run."

"And you're taking someone's car?" Dalton eyed the black 2021 Audi.

Adam shrugged and dropped his gloved hand from the door handle. "I don't have a car."

"I do." Dalton lifted the keys in his hand and a chirp sounded from the dark Jeep he drove while home.

Adam eyed the vehicle like it was a scorpion and stayed where he was.

"Come on, I've already got it warmed up," he coaxed.

"Why?" There went that cute furrow between Adam's brows.

Dalton held back asking what kind of errand would take Adam out in the middle of the night because he had a sneaky suspicion Adam was taking off and Dalton wasn't going to let that happen—not if he could help it.

"I need to run an errand in town myself."

"This late?" Adam's look turned skeptical.

"Yes, so this is perfect." Dalton smiled, trying to appear uncaring.

He backed toward the Jeep, holding the keys dangling in his hands, and kept the smile on his lips. The anxious look in Adam's eyes had him worried, but he'd be damned if he'd show it. Adam didn't need any pressure right now. Dalton had a feeling the man would disappear if pushed too hard.

Adam rubbed a hand against his mouth and slowly followed him. Dalton shoved down his desire to fist pump the air and instead, opened the passenger door with a flourish and a sweep of his arm.

Adam rolled his eyes and Dalton swallowed back the groan that came up in his throat when a smile worked over Adam's full lips. Closing the door, he hoofed it over and slid behind the wheel, cranking up the heat.

"You can drop me at Frazer's Gas," Adam said, buckling his seatbelt.

Not the airport after all, his chest felt light but then he frowned.

"What are you going to do there?" he asked.

Adam gave a deep sigh. "I need some time. To think."

Of course, Adam would need time to think, and the gas station's market and diner was the only thing open this late at night.

"Can you get me some of those wedding cake cookies? I bet they still carry them." He wisely changed the subject.

"Some things never change." Adam's mouth quirked.

"I don't eat the whole box in one sitting anymore," he said.

"Your mom will be pissed."

"Don't tell her." He tossed Adam a smile.

"Right." Adam crossed his arms, but Dalton could tell the man was trying not to laugh.

"Pecan cookies. I can't help it," Dalton argued.

"I know," Adam said with a soft smile. "I remember."

He gave Adam one last smile and then pulled out from the driveway and onto the plowed road.

"What do you do for a living?" he asked and turned the Jeep down the street that would take them to town.

"This and that." Adam evaded.

"What does that mean?"

"Just what I said."

"So, like a handyman?"

"No."

"Then what?" He glanced over and found Adam looking out the window, so he couldn't see the man's face. "Tell me."

"Look, we aren't going down this road. If I thought I was going to get the third degree, I would have taken the car."

"Stolen."

"What?"

From the corner of his eye, he noted Adam's head whipped around. Dalton kept his eyes on the road as they entered town.

"I don't steal," Adam mumbled.

"You don't sound too sure of that."

"Screw you."

He laughed at the outrage in Adam's voice. "Sorry. It's just that you're being deliberately vague."

"Maybe that's because I don't want you to know anything about me."

Squeezing the steering wheel, Dalton stared out the front windshield. The silence in the cab grew thick. When he reached Frazer's parking lot, he stopped the Jeep but didn't park it.

"Dalton… I'm sorry," Adam whispered.

He took a deep breath and turned to face Adam. "I'm the one that's sorry. I just… want to get to know you."

Adam closed his eyes as if he were in pain.

"Don't make any decisions yet," Dalton said hurriedly before Adam could say anything else. "Just think about it."

Adam swallowed and rubbed at his mouth. Those big blue eyes were locked with his.

"Please, just think about it," he whispered, his heart in his throat.

"Okay."

Relief crashed over Dalton, making him lightheaded, and he smiled. "When should I pick you back up?"

"An hour?"

"I'll be here."

Adam slipped out of the Jeep.

"Don't forget my cookies!" he called out before the door shut.

Adam laughed. It was a small one, but Dalton heard it before the door closed. He grinned and then pulled the Jeep out of the parking lot.

❖ ❖ ❖

Dalton came upon the vehicle crash as he approached the motel where he was to meet Farnsworth.

One of the agents wearing an FBI badge stepped up to his vehicle when Dalton rolled down the window.

"Can I help you?"

"I'm supposed to be meeting Agent Farnsworth."

"Dalton Weber?"

"That's me."

"ASAC Farnsworth was in an accident." The man's voice shook. "They're transporting him to the nearest hospital."

Twenty minutes later, Dalton turned away from the apologetic doctor in the hospital waiting room and strode toward the exit doors.

Stopping short of stepping outside into the freezing air, he pulled his phone out and called Ace.

"Did you find Farnsworth?" Ace said right out of the gate and with no hello.

"Yeah." Dalton blew out a hard breath. "He's been murdered."

"Fucking hell," Ace muttered.

The silence stretched over the line.

"When?"

"The Fairbanks field office estimates about two hours ago his SUV was forced off the road," he said, knowing his voice sounded tired as hell.

"You think Sphinx did it?"

"That's what the FBI is saying," he growled.

The FBI agents inside the hospital had been quick to pin the blame on Sphinx.

"Was it a hit and run?"

"According to witnesses, the driver ran Farnsworth off the road. Then got out of his car and shot Farnsworth point-blank in the chest. The Feds found a few dark hairs and a glove at the scene. They're having those tested."

"The gunman left hair and a glove?"

"Supposedly," he muttered, knowing how insane that sounded.

"That doesn't sound like Sphinx," Ace murmured.

Ace had hit the nail on the head, but maybe being on the run was making Sphinx sloppy. Sloppy enough to drop his fucking glove in freezing cold weather? He couldn't see that happening.

"Honestly, Ace? I don't get it. None of this is making any sense. We can't find the list, so it might not exist, and why would Sphinx kill Farnsworth? For what purpose?"

"Farnsworth wanted Sphinx dead," Ace pointed out.

"I still don't buy that Sphinx left hair and his glove at the scene."

"It sounds fishy, but we still need to bring Sphinx in. I'm looking at the FBI field report right now. The charges have changed, and it's no longer only espionage. He's wanted now in connection to the death of Federal Agent Farnsworth and you know what that means."

Yeah, he knew. The warrant for Sphinx would upgrade to dead or alive.

"Take your vacation, let the team know the details, and I'll be in touch the minute Sphinx surfaces," Ace said.

"Copy," Dalton responded automatically to the tone of authority in the ex-Navy Seal's voice.

When Ace gave him word on Sphinx, Dalton would do whatever it took to bring the man to justice.

It looked like the days of talking to Sphinx were over. When Ace ended the call, Dalton sent a short text to Pegasus. In a few words, he explained the situation and told them to stay ready.

This was the hardest part of his job, apprehending fugitives for other agencies. If Sphinx really did kill Farnsworth, then he'd bring him in at all costs.

And if Sphinx resisted?

Dalton would give the order to kill.

CHAPTER FIFTEEN

Adam

THE HUM OF THE TELEVISION HANGING ON THE WALL OVER THE bar was only smothered by the sound of a noisy table of four in the corner of the run-down bar.

He grimaced, shifted on the stool, and wiggled his wet toes in his shoes. His black sneakers were not weatherproof and his toes squished inside his wet, icy socks.

The informant was half an hour late and he already regretted agreeing to the meet at the dive bar not far from Frazer's Gas.

He drained the coffee the bartender had poured and glanced at his watch. He had fifteen minutes before he had to meet Dalton back at the gas station. The plastic bag sitting on the bar crinkled when he grabbed it. He'd picked up two packages of Dalton's favorite cookies.

Paying his tab for the coffee, he gave the bartender an

up-nod and slid from his stool. Buttoning his wool coat, he stepped outside into the frigid night air. A shiver worked its way up his spine and he pulled his gloves on.

The street stood empty save for a few souls braving the frigid weather. Back-to-back storms were on the horizon, the weather app said they'd hit before dawn. Taking his time, he studied each dark figure on the street. It paid to be vigilant. It kept him alive and breathing, and that was the way he liked it.

After a moment, he crossed the snowy street and walked down another road. This one would take him toward the back side of Frazer's. Halfway down the block, he sent a text to Black.

No informant at the meeting place. No package received. Double-check with your contact. I'm going home.

His handler didn't respond, but that was normal. Sometimes, Black didn't get back to him for days. It wouldn't be for much longer, though, and Adam wondered how he'd make a living after he quit. Anything had to be better than this. Living off another's generosity was not something he was proud of. He'd pay every penny back to Leslie. He had skills. Sure, they were military skills, but he could get a job as a security guard, bodyguard, bounty hunter, or even a mercenary. There were plenty of options.

Stay where you are, I'll come get you, Black responded.

Adam frowned at his phone. What the hell was Black doing in Alaska? Why the fuck did Black need him for a job when he was already in the area?

I have a ride, don't bother. Adam fired off the text and shoved the phone back into his coat. The asshole.

Flashing lights reflected off the icy streets ahead, drawing his attention. It appeared to be an accident; crime scene tape surrounded a vehicle that looked to have been run off the road.

A tow truck drove past him, going way too fast, its tires plowing through the white streets. Dirty snow splashed up and he lightly stepped away. The closer he drew parallel to the scene, the more he saw of what remained of the accident.

It looked like a car crash. People drove too fast around here. He passed the crime scene, careful to keep his face hidden inside the collar of his coat. Maybe that was what had happened to the informant? He thought about asking someone about the accident, but decided against it. He couldn't risk blowing his cover, and even if the accident involved Black's informant, the guy would already be at the hospital.

He pulled out his phone and sent another text to Black while he walked.

Accident on Main St. that could be your informant. Check the hospital and get the package from there. I'm going home.

No response to that, so he tucked the burner phone away and pulled his personal cell out. He huffed with a smirk at the funny emoji face Dalton has sent him along with a text: *On my way back to the market. You better have my cookies.*

Frazer's Market came into sight, and he walked along the slippery sidewalk next to the front of the building. All he had to do was wait by the front doors until Dalton came to pick him up and then give the guy his cookies. He didn't need to take whatever Dalton wanted to the next level. The fact of the matter was he couldn't take it to the next level. Not while he was on the run and Dalton was the one after him.

Dalton would arrest him if he found out, of that he had no doubt. Cookies aside, if Dalton knew he was Sphinx, he'd be behind bars in a heartbeat. Why the hell he'd bought the damned treats for the guy was beyond him. Except that cookies made Dalton happy and, well, Adam wanted Dalton happy. Even if he wasn't the one for Dalton, he wanted him to have every happiness.

He glanced at the bag filled with cookies and a snort-laugh emerged from his throat. So many memories came back with these freaking cookies. Dalton had a sweet tooth a mile long and his mother had learned to hide any cookies after baking them because Dalton would eat them.

All of them.

As in... eat every last one of them and leave nothing for the guests. When Dalton had realized his mom was hiding the homemade cookies, he'd coaxed Adam into being his accomplice. Adam would distract Leslie on their weekly shopping trip and Dalton would buy cookies on the sly. Pecan crumbles rolled in white powdered sugar, also called wedding cakes. He remembered the look on Dalton's face when they'd discovered that Frazer's carried the same cookies. He smiled at nothing as the memories rushed up.

What are you doing?

He stopped on the slushy sidewalk, gazing down at the wet slop surrounding his numb, damp feet. A trash can sat to his right and the open road to his left. His heart squeezed as tightly as his fist around the plastic bag.

Just give them to Dalton.

His hand hovered with the bag over the open trash can, but he couldn't let go and clutched the bag against his chest.

What can it hurt? They're only cookies, he reasoned.

Crack!

The bricks from a large gray pillar exploded near his head. The flying debris didn't register at first, which was odd, because he'd been trained for this. In hindsight, he just hadn't thought about dodging bullets here in Alaska.

One of the pillars that sat in front of the store had saved his head from exploding. He scrambled, slipping on the slushy snow, and went down. His knee cracked against the sidewalk with a glancing pain and he lurched upright, the stress of his fall sending the previous bullet graze in his side zipping with pain.

Ducking his head and shoulders, Adam ran in a crouch to take cover behind the next pillar.

"Get back!" he hissed at a woman coming out of the gas station's front entrance. She froze, not understanding.

Adam couldn't take a chance of an innocent being shot and dodged back the other way. No way in hell was he going to return fire in front of the store. Bullets peppered the front of the building, hitting the newspaper stand. Glass shattered and papers flew beneath the barrage. He ran along the building with bullets following, each projectile plunging into the building in his wake.

Skirting a bike rack, he raced down the dark and deserted side of the building and around to the back, hoping like hell his knee held up. The pain was now a distant throb. It was his side that worried him; a wet warmth ran down his side and soaked his pants.

Hopefully, there would be a delivery van or something where he could take cover. He pulled his weapon as he slowed into a jog. He had one full clip in his nine-millimeter and another tucked into his jacket. Reaching a van, he stepped into the dark shadows and leaned his back against the cold metal. Fog filled the brisk air with every breath he took and he tried to slow his breathing, his mind racing for the next steps.

Tires sloshed through the melting snow and he braced himself, but it wasn't the bad guys.

Dalton's big black Jeep rolled into view.

Adam froze in the shadows. Maybe if he stayed very still, Dalton wouldn't see him.

In the next instant, the Jeep pulled up to the shadowed spot where he stood.

The window rolled down.

"Get in!"

He looked at Dalton through the open window and then glanced at the dark road that led out of town.

The Jeep passenger door popped open.

"Get the fuck in the Jeep, Adam," Dalton barked across the distance, his voice dropping deeper than normal. The words were a command.

Urgent. Lethal. Brooking no argument. In fact, Adam thought that Dalton would chase him down if he tried to run.

Fuck, shit, damn it.

CHAPTER SIXTEEN

Dalton

AT FIRST, HE DIDN'T THINK ADAM WAS GOING TO JUMP IN. IN THE next instance, Adam leaped into the Jeep and slammed the door.

"Get down and stay down." Dalton reached over and put his hand on Adam's head and shoved downward. Adam slipped off the seat and onto the passenger floorboard and curled into a small ball.

Dalton eased his foot on the gas. He wanted to slam down the pedal, but it would only send the Jeep into a spinout, which was not an option. Once the Jeep gained traction and hit the salted streets, he floored it. The back fishtailed in what remained of the slush, but the tires caught the salt and the vehicle lurched forward.

Bullets pinged, hitting the tail end of his Jeep. Two darkly dressed figures ran into the street. Through the rearview window, Dalton could see them raise their guns. Dalton yanked the wheel and drove the Jeep up on the snow-covered grass of a corner lot. The tires caught and slid off the curb with a bounce. He spun the wheel the other way and took the narrow alley to the left. It was filled with snow, and he floored it and took the next alley to the right. By the time he was done zigzagging through a maze of alleys and streets, the bad guys had no hope of finding them.

"It's clear," he growled at the curled-up, dark lump on the floorboard.

Adam didn't respond.

Nor did he move.

Fear blasted through his chest and he jerked the wheel and slammed the Jeep into park next to a trash can and killed the lights.

"Adam?"

Dalton reached over and gripped the heavy wool coat and tugged.

Adam was dead weight.

"Fuck!"

Dalton jumped out of the Jeep and ran around to the passenger door and yanked it open. He reached beneath Adam's arms and lifted him up. In the overhead light, blood covered the pale leather seats.

"Adam, Adam," he crooned, pulling the slighter man close. Feeling the warmth of his body. He placed his ear and face down next to Adam's mouth and choked on the wave of relief when warm air touched his face. Easing Adam to his side on the seat, he curled the man's knees and made sure his feet were away from the door before shutting it. Racing around, he jumped behind the wheel and lifted Adam's head to rest on the center console, its soft leather a pillow for his head.

Back on the road, Dalton's mind raced. Hospital? No.

He punched in a number and impatiently waited for it to ring.

"Dalton? Long time no hear."

Dr. Basil Washburn answered on the first ring, and Dalton explained the situation. Well, what he knew of the situation. Suspected gunshot wound.

"Harbor General is right there," Basil said.

"I think that's the first place they'll look for us."

Silence filled the line.

"Please, Basil."

"My place and fucking hurry."

Dalton punched in another number and floored the Jeep in the doc's direction.

"Dalton?" Ace might have been sleeping, but he was alert when he answered the phone.

"Someone just tried to kill a friend of mine." Dalton cut right to the chase and filled Ace in on the events since leaving the hospital.

"Where are you?"

"Heading to a doctor friend. I can't take Ada…my friend back home."

"Does your family need protection?"

"Yes," he said without hesitation.

"On it. Give me their address," Ace ordered.

Dalton rattled off the mansion's address, and Ace ended the call with a promise to call him back.

He kept his free hand on Adam's curly hair, fingering the silk-like strands.

The rage built.

With his left hand, he squeezed the steering wheel in a death grip while his right hand wound its way through soft, dark curls before slipping down to cup Adam's cheek.

Whoever had shot at Adam was a dead man.

And Dalton was going to fire the fatal shot.

The only thing that kept him from hunting down the fucking bastard and ending his life was the soft warmth of Adam's cheek beneath his palm.

* * *

The quiet beeping of the heart monitor was calming and he could have stood there forever in Basil's spare room, watching Adam sleep.

Basil had other plans, though.

"This way," the doc said, wiping Adam's blood from his hands before leaving the room.

The place was massive, filled with light, and fashionably decorated for the holiday. Garland and lights draped over a wooden mantel and a seven-foot-tall tree was decorated to the hilt. Clove and cinnamon drifted on the air and Basil's golden Labrador raised its head from the rug before the fire and blinked at him sleepily. Dalton stopped and ran his fingers over Biscuit's big head.

"Hey, old boy." The dog must have been fifteen by now and it showed in the gray around his ears and muzzle.

Dalton then caught up with his friend in the bright, lavish kitchen with its white countertops and stainless-steel appliances. Wicker and splashes of red accessories lay scattered around as if Basil had been in the middle of cooking when he called.

Basil washed his hands at the sink before pulling down two coffee mugs from the cabinet over the granite counter.

Basil hadn't changed much in the year since Dalton had last seen him. They'd served in the Marines together as Raiders, and afterward, Basil had done mercenary work with him for about a year and then dropped out. The doc now worked as a part-time surgeon in the nearby hospital.

"Your friend will live, but that bullet wound in his side isn't fresh. It didn't happen tonight. So, what's going on?"

"I don't fucking know." Dalton sent his fingers through his hair and then took the cup of hot coffee Basil held out. It warmed his cold hands and he gripped it like a lifeline.

"I'm on a case. I can't go into details, but the guy I'm after is dangerous. We suspect that he killed someone I worked with and now Adam was shot at while waiting for me."

How the fuck did Sphinx know where he was and, more importantly, how the hell did Sphinx know about Adam?

Why did Adam have a bullet wound in his side? Was that the reason he was really here in Alaska? All Dalton had were more questions. Questions that only Adam could answer.

"You still have that cabin?"

"I do." Basil eyed him over the rim of his cup. "But it's occupied."

"Shit." Dalton let out a harsh sigh.

"I have the beach house."

"Yeah?" Dalton grew hopeful.

"Yeah." Basil lifted a set of keys from a peg over the sink and handed it to him.

"Is he safe to travel?" He shot a worried glance toward the bedroom.

"Yes, after the sedative wears off."

"Can I borrow your truck? I'd leave you my Jeep, but I don't think you should drive it."

Sphinx, or whoever was after Dalton, would know that Jeep by now. He tried to remember the size of the darkly dressed figures in his rearview mirror, but he couldn't decide if one of them could have been Sphinx. And another fact was that Sphinx worked alone.

"Yeah, leave the Jeep in the garage where it is and use my pickup," Basil offered.

"Thanks, Basil, I owe you one."

"More like three, but who's counting?" The man smirked.

Back in Adam's room, Dalton took a seat in the armchair next to the bed and sipped his coffee. Somewhere in Adam's coat, hanging on a treadmill in the corner of the room, a phone rang.

Shoving to his feet, he searched through the pockets and found Adam's cell phone.

Adam's cell was silent.

The ringing continued, and in the inside pocket of Adam's coat, he pulled out another phone. It looked like a typical burner phone.

He frowned and studied the phone before pushing the button to stop it. The room rang with silence save for the heart monitor Basil still had at the house. The man's mom had convalesced at home before she'd passed away a few years ago.

Dalton held the button down on both phones, powering them off. When he tucked them back into Adam's wool coat, his hand met metal.

His gaze settled on a sleeping Adam.

Why would Adam need two phones?

And a gun.

CHAPTER SEVENTEEN

Adam

ROLLING TO HIS SIDE, PAIN LANCED THROUGH HIM AND AN ACHE set up in his knee. A lethargic sounding groan left his lips before he could swallow it down.

"Adam?"

He blinked open his lids to a bright, blurry room and the outline of a dark figure hovering over him. The voice was Dalton's deep rumble.

"Yeah," he croaked, getting up onto his elbow only to slide back down into the bed's softness. "I'm awake."

"Easy."

A hand caressed soothingly over his forehead, brushing back the strands of hair from his eyes. Fingertips lingered on his cheek and then trailed down the side of his neck. His pulse thundered beneath the tips of fingers he knew as well as his own.

He blinked again and Dalton's face swam into focus and then the room beyond. It was not his bedroom at the Weber home. Brightness washed through this particular room and bounced off of light blue walls. Ribbons of sunlight filtered through white slatted blinds, dappling the buttercup yellow bedspread draped over him and the bed.

"Where are we?" Adam brushed a palm over the bedspread and again got an elbow beneath him. "What happened?"

"We're at my friend's beach house," Dalton said, helping him sit up.

Once upright, Adam arranged the bedspread, and Dalton lifted a glass filled with orange juice from the nightstand. The straw was held to his lips and he obediently took several swallows of the sweet drink. It went a long way in clearing the fog from his brain.

"As for what happened, we'll go over all that after you eat something."

The night before came rushing back. Someone had shot at him. Had it been only last night? Maybe he'd been out longer. He glanced toward the window.

"How long have we been here?"

"Since early this morning." Dalton placed the half-empty juice cup on the nightstand.

"What time is it?" He felt like a parrot, asking so many questions.

"One o'clock in the afternoon."

"Where's my jacket?" Surely Black had to have called? His handler was probably worried sick.

"In the hall closet," Dalton said, locking hard gold eyes on him.

The smile on Adam's lips faded beneath the glittering gaze.

"What?" he whispered, licking at his suddenly dry lips.

"You have a bullet wound."

"Well, yeah, they shot at me."

Dalton squinted at him, and his mouth pressed flat before an expression of disappointment swam through the man's eyes.

"That wound is older than last night."

Shit, damn it. Adam glanced away and plucked at the bedspread.

"If you're in trouble, you know you can come to me."

"Can I?"

Dalton looked confused and hurt all rolled into one. "You of all people should know that."

Silence ran through the room, lingered, and then increased when he stayed silent.

"I've made breakfast. I'll see you at the table. The kitchen is down the hall, make a left. Bathroom is through there," Dalton clipped out, pointed to a door off of the room, and walked out.

The door shut with a snap, which spoke louder than the hurt in Dalton's whiskey-colored eyes.

"Damn it," he muttered and sat up with a grimace.

He shoved the yellow bedspread out of his way and sat up on the edge of the bed. Gazing down at the pajamas he wore, he tossed a glance at the door. He hoped Dalton had gotten his looking in because that was all he was going to get. Still, thinking of Dalton undressing him and tucking him into pajamas sent a shiver of desire down his spine. Rolling his eyes at his nonsense, he eased from the bed.

Finding his coat was paramount, and he located it hanging in the closet. His phones had been powered down, but his gun was still inside. He tucked it and the phones away in the nightstand and hobbled into the bathroom without any mishaps.

Twenty minutes later, he was freshly showered and wearing a pair of sweatpants, rolled at the waist, and a t-shirt that was miles too big for him. He pulled on the pair of thick socks he'd found with the clothes sitting on a chair in the bathroom. The unwrapped toothbrush had been a bonus.

Damn…he felt almost human. He hadn't passed out like that ever and chalked it up to his lack of sleep over the past few months. He finger-combed his wildly curly hair in an effort to tame it.

"Welp, that's about as good as it's going to get." He sighed at the springy black strands.

He found Dalton in a wide, sunny kitchen with accessories rivaling the yellow in the bedroom. The owner must have a thing for brightness because the whole room looked like something out of a country kitchen magazine in the middle of a sunflower summer.

"I know, Mom. Yes, no, okay. Love you too," Dalton's deep voice filled the kitchen.

Adam stepped into the doorway.

"Yes, he's right here." Dalton held out the phone.

Taking the phone, he put it to his ear. The song "White Christmas" was playing.

"Adam? Oh, Adam, honey, are you okay?" Leslie's voice was filled with worry. It made his chest hurt.

"Of course," he murmured, sliding into a chair.

"Dalton told me you got caught in the crosshairs of his work! Oh, that makes me so mad."

His eyes flew up to Dalton. The man smirked and continued to nurse his cup of coffee at the table.

"I'm okay." He squeezed the phone.

"I love you," she said fiercely.

"I love you too," he murmured, holding Dalton's gaze before he ended the call and passed him the phone.

The white-washed kitchen table looked decadent. Two chunky white plates were piled high with eggs, sausage, and hashbrowns. His stomach growled as he slid into the vacant chair.

"Coffee?"

"Sure. Your mom's not mad at you, is she?" Sometimes, because of his childhood, Leslie treated him kinder than the scolding she'd give her own children.

Dalton picked up the pot sitting on a warmer on the table and filled a large mug that sat near his plate before sliding creamer and sugar closer.

"She'll be fine. I told her to give us a few days."

"Days?" Dalton wanted to stay here a few days?

"As long as we're home for Christmas," Dalton finished.

"Right," he smiled. Leslie was all about family and the holiday. God, he'd missed that. He gazed at the food arranged on the table and a freshly showered Dalton.

It all felt so domestic. Too domestic, and he almost bailed back to his room, but the company and the smell of sausage called to him. Screw it, he was hungry. He dug into the food, eating like it was his last meal, but it kept him from talking.

"You can have seconds."

He paused after shoveling another bite of sausage and egg into his mouth and darting a look at Dalton from beneath his lashes. He found the man's eyes locked on his face before dropping down to his mouth.

Those damned butterflies lurched in his stomach and his traitorous cock twitched beneath the soft material of the sweats, reminding him that he wasn't wearing briefs. His breath caught and Dalton's pupils expanded. Quickly, he returned his gaze to his plate and took another bite of food.

"Talk to me, Adam. How did you get that gunshot wound?"

He took several swallows of the sweet coffee to chase down the eggs that were lodged in his throat.

How the hell was he going to explain getting shot?

Stall.

Stall like a motherfucker.

"That's a long and funny story," he said with a small laugh.

"I've got time."

"Maybe I don't," he tossed back.

Dalton glanced out the window at the snow-packed fields.

"It's a long walk back to town."

"I'll borrow your jeep."

"The Jeep isn't here. I borrowed a friend's truck and have the keys."

He swept his eyes around the room. Maybe the owner would have another car or bike, or hell, he'd take snowshoes at this point.

"In my pocket," Dalton added. "Now, talk to me."

"Why!"

"Because I'm asking you to."

"You're so annoying. Like a bulldog with a bone."

"Tell me."

"Oh, for fuck's sake." He stabbed at a sausage link. "I work for a top-secret organization! I can't tell you which one or I'd have to kill you. Anyways… some very bad men are after me for something I didn't do and they shot me."

Dalton's brows had furrowed during his rant. The man's face looked like a thundercloud had taken up residence.

What the hell? Should he not have blurted all that out? Too bad, Dalton had asked for it.

"You said you wanted the truth," he continued flippantly and shrugged before scooping a large bite of hashbrowns into his mouth.

"Are you fucking with me?" Dalton asked in a really quiet tone, too quiet.

"Would I do that?" He flashed Dalton a cheeky smile.

"Are you lying?" Dalton growled, his voice kind of strangled. Like, he was ready to start yelling and it made Adam want to really smile.

So, he did; his lips stretched upward, letting the humor he felt show in his eyes. Of course, that led to Dalton getting the wrong impression.

It really wasn't his fault Dalton thought he was lying.

"Look…I'm not obligated to tell you a freaking thing." He pointed his fork with the sausage wobbling on the prongs at Dalton and squinted, hoping that by giving the guy the stink-eye, Dalton would stop with the inquisition.

"If you're in trouble, I can help." The hurt that swam in Dalton's eyes made his chest ache.

Adam softened.

"I swear, if I need your help, I will ask you," he said, keeping his voice quiet and sincere, letting Dalton know by his tone and words he meant what he said.

Did he though?

Would he ask Dalton for help when shit came down to the wire?

No.

He couldn't forget that Dalton wanted him dead.

CHAPTER EIGHTEEN

Dalton

H E COULDN'T LOOK AWAY WHEN ADAM ATE THE SAUSAGE ON THE end of his fork.

Clearing his throat, Dalton fumbled for his coffee cup.

"So…" Adam licked at his bottom lip. "Why do you think I was shot at last night?"

"You were caught in the crossfire of a very bad man who wants me dead."

"What?" Adam's eyebrows flew up and his eyes widened. "Are you lying?" Adam tossed his earlier words back at him.

"No." He scowled. "I don't lie."

"Yes, you do." Adam picked up his plate and walked to the sink. Water rushed from the faucet, and the muscles in Adam's back were rigid. "You lied to me when we were younger."

The harshly spoken words soured his stomach.

"What?" he croaked, trying to collect his response.

"You said we'd be together forever." Adam spun and sat his back to the counter. Those blue eyes were hard and brittle, locked on him. "You lied about that. You broke it off."

"Adam... I told you I'm sorry." He raked his fingers through his hair, sighed, and glanced away.

"Why did you do it?" Adam hissed.

"If you're looking for excuses... like someone made me do it or I was forced in some way, you're not going to find any," he rasped out over a suddenly tight throat. "I was stupid, young, and didn't know what I wanted." He swallowed. "And I didn't know what I had... until I lost it."

"So..." Adam squinted at him. "You broke up with me because you were young and dumb?"

"I was scared for you. For us." Dalton admitted. "I was training to be a Raider. That's a dangerous job and on top of that, I wasn't out."

"But you were out at home." Adam's brow furrowed.

"I know, but I wasn't out in the military. You of all people know we keep our mouths shut."

"Of course! I didn't go blabbing either!" Adam tossed up his hands. "But I was okay just being with you on your leave time. We were going to make a life when you got out."

He'd spent his whole life up to that point and after his fuck-up with Adam knowing what he wanted and who he'd wanted it with. A few days of being away from Adam had gutted him, and it took a month for additional leave time to kick in and he'd taken shit from his commander to get it. Of course, by then, it had been too late. Adam had been gone. Gone from the house and gone from his life. He swallowed around a tightened throat.

"I'm not saying it makes any sense what I did. I was young and fucking scared."

The words rang out loudly in the room and then faded, leaving silence in their wake.

"I'd give anything to take it all back," he went on quietly. "I came back, but you were gone."

"You weren't taking my calls. You'd abandoned me, so I left."

"I know. I'm so sorry, Adam. I came to Randy's funeral hoping to apologize to you, but I saw you with your fiancé."

"Why didn't you find me sooner than Randy's funeral?" Hurt swam in Adam's voice and was etched on the beautiful plains of his face.

"You were still in the service."

"I had one more tour." Adam nodded, rubbing at his lips. "What about after that? I got out of the Army five years ago."

"I thought you were happy with someone else." Dalton's chest ached.

"I ended it with Michael." Adam wrapped his arms around his slender form.

"I got your number," Dalton went on doggedly. "I called you every year on your birthday."

"You called me?" Adam rubbed a hand at his mouth. "I didn't get any messages."

"I didn't leave any," he admitted, feeling like a fool.

"Of course. I think I remember a heavy breather," Adam said flatly.

"Yeah, I fucked that up too." He sighed and glanced away. "Believe it or not, I don't always have the answers."

"You mean you aren't always a badass?" Adam teased.

"Hey now, don't get carried away."

Adam softened further, and one side of his lips curled

upward. A tiny light danced in his blue eyes. "You are the worst."

"I am. Can you forgive me?" He pushed back from the table and stood slowly. He half expected Adam to bolt as he approached.

"I forgive you." Adam held up a hand and he halted in his tracks. "That doesn't mean I want to pick up where we left off."

The pain in Dalton's chest grew and he nodded. He couldn't blame Adam.

"I mean, how could I ever trust that you wouldn't come home someday and break it off with me?" Adam mused as if working it all out in that gorgeous head of his.

"I've grown up since then. I'm not a scared boy any longer."

Adam licked at his bottom lip, swallowed, and then rubbed his hands over the baggy pair of sweats. Adam wanted him. Only, something was holding him back. Maybe it was the unknown.

He took a chance.

"I want the whole package. The house, the husband, the kids."

"And you want that with me?" Adam questioned, sounding skeptical. "We're strangers," Adam said impatiently. "I mean, how do you even know you're going to like me now? You're going off a feeling from when we were kids."

"I know." Dalton sighed.

"Someone needs to be the voice of reason here." Adam's voice grew breathy.

Dalton took another step closer and the pulse in Adam's throat jumped. Adam's lips parted and his chest lifted. His own body hardened, his need for Adam off the fucking Richter scale. But he had to face the facts, he didn't really know Adam any longer and Adam didn't know him. So then, how could one person be so attracted to another? It was fate, and even with so much time apart, he and Adam were meant to be together.

"Let's... hang out."

"Hang out?" Adam echoed in disbelief.

"Mhmm. You know, decorate for Christmas, drink hot chocolate, and make snow angels." Fuck if he didn't sound corny as shit, but right then, he didn't care. All he cared about was having Adam close. Keeping Adam safe.

"Does your friend have Christmas decorations?"

"Yes."

Adam tipped his head as if thinking about it. "I've already helped decorate a mansion."

"Mhmm."

"I might be tired."

"We can rest in between."

"We'd need to get a tree." Adam gestured to the empty living room that sat across from the kitchen's island.

Dalton smiled, drawing closer and closer the more they argued. Once he was standing in front of Adam and the connection between them was causing both of their breathing to increase, Adam placed a palm flat to his chest.

His heart jumped beneath Adam's touch.

"One kiss..." Dalton breathed.

"Technically, this would be kiss number two," Adam whispered, his voice all but gone.

"Then two more kisses."

A laugh huffed from Adam's full, parted lips and Dalton muffled it with his mouth.

When Adam moaned, Dalton followed suit. When Adam's lips parted, Dalton thrust his tongue in and toyed with Adam's own.

Adam fisted his hair and Dalton came up for air, easing his lips from Adam's mouth.

"Better find an axe," Adam said.

"Axe?" He drew back farther to gaze down into Adam's face.

"Something to cut down the tree." Adam's lips pursed.

"Right…" He swallowed. "Tree."

Adam grinned and spun away from him. "That's right, you promised me decorations."

He groaned and adjusted himself.

"And if you really want to get to know me," Adam said, tossing a glance over his shoulder, "you won't do it with sex."

"But sex would help," Dalton pointed out. Yeah, he'd grumbled that, but it was worth it to hear Adam's laughter.

CHAPTER NINETEEN

Three days later.
Adam

"Not that one!" He huffed out a laugh when Dalton pointed to a Charlie Brown tree.

Dalton's eyebrows lifted. "No?"

Adam shook his head and pointed to the bigger, thicker tree next to the tiny one. He couldn't keep the smile off his face.

"I only need branches for a wreath." Adam rolled his eyes.

Everything seemed so normal, here at the beach house, which wasn't really on the beach; it was five miles inland and sat on a snow-filled rocky cliff. The silence was so thick it was soothing.

Here, it didn't feel like someone was trying to kill him. As much as Dalton wanted to think whoever shot at him was after Dalton, Adam knew better. Those bullets that punched into the brick of Frazer's Market were meant for him.

He'd tried over the past several days to come up with a plan. A plan that included telling Dalton who he was. Maybe after he got to know this new and seemingly improved Dalton, he could find a way to drop the bomb.

Oh, by the way, that guy you've been trying to kill? I'm him.

Only, there never seemed to be a right time to tell Dalton his real story, and between the flirting, kisses, and all-around groping, his mind had been elsewhere. When they talked about the past and good times, he hadn't wanted to ruin what little time they had left together.

Now that he stood outside and away from the cozy house, Adam could think clearly. He sighed, white puffs of air escaping into the cold.

Who was he kidding? Thinking clearly around Dalton was a myth.

Take now for instance…

Dalton was cutting fern fronds for a front door wreath. They'd already cut down a tree from the small patch of trees next to the house the first day and had spent hours decorating it.

The muscles of Dalton's forearms rippled with the work he was doing. Each tattoo seemed to gleam in the bright sun's light. There were only a few hours of daylight at this time of year and it was still fucking cold, but the small trip had been worth it.

Dalton was a vision even in snow pants and jacket, and much like he'd been doing for days, Adam contemplated taking Dalton up on his offer of sex. They could have sex without getting all emotionally tangled up. Couldn't they?

Dalton wanted a family, he reminded himself. Would that be so bad? Hell yes, it would, seeing that he was the one on the run and his life was kind of complicated at the moment with people wanting him dead.

It was the wrong time for them.

Again.

A lump grew in his throat and his eyes burned as they roamed over Dalton.

Adam reached down and collected snow before packing it into a snowball, then he launched it at Dalton and it smacked the man on the shoulder.

Dalton stopped cutting branches and gazed at him across the short distance.

Adam licked his lips and, not hiding his desire, he held Dalton's gaze across the distance.

The man's hand squeezed around the shear's handle.

"I thought you wanted to take things slow," Dalton rasped.

"I lied," he croaked back, letting the building hunger reflect in his eyes. "I can't give you tomorrow, but I can give you today."

He had to make it clear to Dalton that they didn't have a future.

"Okay," Dalton said slowly, picked up the bunch of branches, and walked toward him. "I'll take what I can get."

"It's nonnegotiable." Adam bit his lip and turned back toward the house. "And I'm still mad at you."

"Still?"

He smiled at the whine in Dalton's question. Hiding his grin, Adam opened the front door so Dalton could carry the branches inside.

"Yes, still. You don't get to dump me, show back up years later, and think you can pick up where we left off."

A thump sounded on the kitchen table when Dalton dropped the shears and branches.

"Don't forget the apology part," Dalton said huskily.

"That's the only reason we're standing here." Adam tipped his chin.

"I want more than sex."

"I'd take what you can get if I were you."

"You're not me." Dalton moved closer.

Adam took a slow step back.

Dalton's eyes narrowed.

Adam's heart slammed against his rib cage, and he shuffled down the hallway. Dalton leaped forward and he felt the man's hands close on his jacket. Adam laughed and slipped out of the coat, leaving it dangling in Dalton's fist. Adam wobbled forward, hurrying down the hallway—as much as his knee would allow, to the bedroom. He slammed through the door and turned, favoring his side.

Dalton crashed in behind him, breathing hard. Stalking forward, Adam fisted Dalton's shirt and jerked him close.

"We have tonight," Adam whispered, pulling Dalton's head down.

"Tonight is good enough."

The words *"for now"* weren't spoken, but Adam heard them as clear as a bell. Dalton wasn't giving up; he could tell by the glittering, intense light in the man's eyes.

It was going to be Adam's turn to break Dalton's heart.

He shoved that thought away and closed the distance between their mouths and kissed the first, last, and only love of his life.

Dalton still doesn't know who you are.

Adam told the voice in his head to shut the hell up and swept his tongue inside of Dalton's mouth. The big man moaned and his hands gripped his hips hard. The harder the better, and he moaned back.

There'd be plenty of time to tell Dalton everything.

Later, though, much, much later.

"Fuck me," he ordered, nipping at Dalton's jaw.

So help him, God, he had neither the will nor the desire to deny them both any longer.

Dalton closed his big hands around his ass and lifted. Adam wrapped his legs and arms around Dalton, who clutched him close. Holding him as if he never wanted to let him go. Kissing along Dalton's neck and jaw, Adam left marks on the man's neck before sliding from Dalton's grip.

Putting a hand up, he kept Dalton from following. Once he gained enough distance, he worked at the buttons of his own shirt. Dalton's eyes were riveted on him as Adam shoved his shirt from his shoulders and let it fall away before starting on the string of his borrowed sweatpants. He'd discovered a few days earlier that he and the absent Basil wore the same size clothes.

Taking his time, he let the sweats fall from his hips. He'd dreamed of this moment and wouldn't be rushed.

Dalton's gaze devoured him, and he was glad he'd kept in shape. Even when Dalton's eyes flickered and darkened when they ran over the small white bandage covering the bullet wound in his side, nothing could dampen the heat growing in the big man's gaze.

Wearing only tight black briefs, Adam backed up until his ass bumped against the wall. Then he slipped a hand down his chest and abs and through the small treasure trail, before dipping his fingers slowly beneath the edge of the tight briefs.

Adam swept a glance up through thick lashes and a sound, much like a growl, erupted from Dalton's throat.

"There may not be supplies," Adam challenged, pulling at his cock hidden beneath the material.

"There damn well better be," Dalton rasped and then

yanked his shirt up and over his head before shucking off his jeans.

A nearly naked Dalton was stunning, and Adam moaned at the ink that covered most of Dalton's chest, arms, neck, and back; Dalton was a vision of art.

The devil gave him a rakish smile and stalked toward the bathroom.

"Ah-ha!"

Triumphant, Dalton returned in seconds with both condoms and lube.

"How long have you known those were there?" he smirked.

"Three days?"

"Lucky," he said with a smile.

"My middle name."

Dalton advanced on him.

CHAPTER TWENTY

Dalton

Swallowing thickly, Dalton shoved his briefs down his legs.

Adam's gaze roamed over his chest, arms, and neck, taking in the ink that covered his body. The man's eyes landed on his left pec and studied the tattoo there.

Dalton was proud of his ink and his cock thickened, growing impossibly harder beneath Adam's approving gaze. Dalton's dick jerked, thrusting from his body when Adam's eyes flickered over his abs and then lingered on his cock.

Dalton hungrily roamed his eyes over Adam and the hand the man had shoved into his tight black briefs. Adam was making no secret about stroking himself and it was driving him fucking crazy.

Instead of stalking closer, Dalton tossed the condoms and lube on the nightstand. Snapping up a condom, he tore the package with his teeth, keeping his eyes locked on Adam and his teasing hand.

He pulled at the head of his dick. Adam's pupils exploded, his eyes flying wide open. Dalton smirked, then bit back a moan as he stroked himself in time to Adam's own hand movements.

Finally, he lowered the condom to his dick, and then he paused.

"Fucking put it on," Adam ordered with a breathy voice, yanking at the dick hidden in his briefs.

Dalton could see the rise and swell of the tip and length of Adam's cock. The man was hands down the sexiest fucking thing he'd ever seen. And he could have kicked his own ass for letting him go, but that was then and this was now and while Adam was here, Dalton was going to take advantage of every way possible to get Adam to stick around.

Dalton rolled on the condom and dumped lube in his hand before tossing the bottle on the nearby dresser. He stroked over his covered cock, imagining being buried deep in Adam.

They belonged together. Hands down. And he was going to do everything in his power to get Adam to recommit to him. He wasn't going to fuck this up a second time. Like he'd told Adam, he wasn't the scared little boy he'd been. He was a man and he wanted Adam with every fiber of his being. Sure, he'd hesitated for the past several fucking years because he'd thought Adam had moved on, but seeing him in his parents' home had reignited every ounce of his feelings. Adam felt the same, he was sure of it.

His eyes landed on Adam's stroking hand, and he had to squeeze his own cock to fight off the orgasm threatening to roll over him.

"Oh, fuck yeah," Adam breathed and slowly slid those

tight, dark briefs down to free his cock. Once freed, Adam teased his fingers around the head, jerking and playing.

Fuck! Dalton groaned and continued to pull at his dick.

"The past few days have been torture," Adam said, licking at his lips and tugging on his cock.

Dalton could have readily come just watching Adam.

"I was wooing you."

Adam's laugh was so fucking sexy. "Consider me wooed."

Grabbing the lube from the dresser, Adam dumped some on his fingers and fingered his own ass with the slick lube. Was Adam slipping in one finger or two? With lips parted and panting breaths, Adam got himself ready.

Dalton could only stand it for so long. After another minute, he'd had enough and growled at the little tease. Not really little, though, as Adam was six feet. Not as tall as his own six feet five, but Adam was fucking ripped. Washboard abs showed definition and the fact that Adam worked out beyond what was normal was a turn-on in itself. Adam had ink as well, and Dalton let his gaze linger on the bright and fresh-looking tattoo over the man's heart.

He roamed forward—enough was enough. Adam appeared to have had enough of the waiting as well and kicked off the dark briefs that hung around one ankle.

Dalton cupped Adam's ass cheeks in both hands. Adam slipped his arms up around his neck and climbed him. Those long legs wrapped around Dalton's waist with Adam's cock and balls grinding against his stomach.

The kiss turned hungry, and they traded nips, nibbles, and tongue-tasting until he was lightheaded from lack of air.

"Fuck," Dalton growled, yanking his head back and sucking in huge gulps of air.

Adam moaned and roamed his mouth along his jaw, tonguing over the ink found along Dalton's neck.

Gripping beneath Adam's thighs, he took a step forward until Adam's back hit the wall.

"Yes, yes," Adam ordered, hands gripping at his shoulders, legs squeezing tightly around his waist, the man's cock caught between them.

For a second, Dalton held still, thinking of adding a finger of his own to get Adam ready.

"Bed?"

"No. Fuck me now. I need you." Adam bit out at his mouth again, thrusting his tongue and grinding against him.

"Fuuuuck," he groaned and slipped Adam's legs over his arms so he could grasp the man's ass and hold him open. Adam was completely exposed and Dalton slid his cock against the tight ring of resistance, brushing back and forth against Adam's hole.

"Yes!" Adam's head rolled back and forth against the wall.

Dalton ran his mouth up the column of Adam's throat and pushed into his body.

"Oh, fuck yes," Adam panted, eyes half-closed.

They'd always been good together, but this…this was fucking nirvana and Dalton could have stayed like this forever with his cock inside of the tight confines of Adam's body.

Gripping Adam's rounded ass cheeks, Dalton squeezed and plunged his dick home time and again. His fingers dug into Adam's cheeks as he lifted and thrust, setting up a hungry rhythm.

And for the first time in a long time, Dalton let the troubles of his mission fade away in Adam's embrace.

CHAPTER TWENTY-ONE

Adam

Hooking his legs over Dalton's arms, Adam hung on.
Dalton pushed between Adam's splayed ass, shoving his back to the wall, and pounded his cock deep inside.

Dalton's long, hard, and beautiful dick plunged inside and with each thrust, Dalton pushed him higher up on the wall. Large hands stretched and held him open, and Adam closed his eyes.

Tossing his head from side to side, a moan pulled from his throat. Sweat covered their bodies, and Dalton's skin grew wet beneath his hands.

The tip of his own dick brushed repeatedly against Dalton's hard stomach, setting up an ache inside.

Adam hung on when Dalton lifted his ass higher, cupping him in his big hands. That right there was a huge turn-on, how Dalton could handle him so easily. Dalton began thrusting again, but this time, Adam's cock bounced in the air.

He groaned at the loss of touch to his dick as it freely bounced between them with every one of Dalton's thrusts. Clutching at Dalton's shoulders, Adam couldn't reach for it and a shiver ran up his spine.

Dalton's cock pegged him, sending another shockwave through Adam's body. His balls grew tight, his cock bounced, and Adam fucking swore he was going to come without touching himself.

"Oh fuck!" Oh yeah, he was going to come! "Oh shit! Oh fuck!" His cock exploded and he doubled up as much as he could. Not able to curl forward, he could only shudder and moan as hot seed shot from his swollen dick in white ropes across his stomach.

"Nnngh." The sound ripped from Dalton, who growled loudly, thrusting hard and sporadically until slamming into him.

Dalton's whole body stiffened, jerked with a few more thrusts, and then grew still.

Easing forward, Dalton drew Adam into his arms and buried his face against his neck. Adam ran his fingers over the man's sweat-soaked inked shoulders and moved his short nails down Dalton's back and then up through the hair at his nape.

Adam caressed his hair as Dalton fought for breath. Dalton had always fucked him as if he were the only man on earth. Adam's chest squeezed and his eyes stung.

Whiskey-colored eyes suddenly caught his when Dalton lifted his head. Sweat dripped, darkening Dalton's hair.

The hand at his ass slowly released him and Adam slipped his feet to the floor, his legs feeling like Jell-O.

Dalton stepped back and Adam kept going down to the floor. He knelt on his discarded sweatpants and pulled the condom from Dalton's dick. Adam tossed it toward the can in the corner, not caring if it made it or not. He licked at his lips before licking at the crown of Dalton's gleaming cock.

"What's the sense of condoms if you're going to eat my come?" Dalton rasped.

"I'm negative," he croaked back.

"Me too," Dalton said.

They probably should have had that conversation before right then, but fuck it. He flicked out his tongue and licked at the crown of Dalton's still hard cock before closing his mouth around the head and sucking.

"Fuuuck," Dalton growled, curling forward and placing one bent arm to the wall. Looking up, he could see that Dalton's eyes were glued to what his mouth was doing. Holding Dalton's gaze, Adam took the cock inch by inch down his throat before pulling off and teasing the head with his tongue.

Dalton's cock was beautiful, thick, and quite long. The flared head was red and swollen. Adam tongued around the edges and then poked into the slit at the top before slipping the tip back into his mouth. The noises coming from Dalton made the work worth it. Plus, the bonus of having his mouth fucked did it for him. Sucking on the tip of Dalton's cock, he reached down and stroked his own growing hardness.

"Fuck yeah, touch yourself." Dalton released a hoarse groan and planted both hands against the wall.

Slipping his wet lips up and down the rock-hard shaft, Adam picked up the pace on his own throbbing dick, twisting and stroking. He shoved down on Dalton's cock, taking him to the root, and stayed there,

Dalton's harsh breathing swam over his head.

Slowly, he slid off the dick until he was only sucking on the head again and tongued the slit. He toyed with the edge of the vein that ran beneath the flared, swollen head and licked it with the flat of his tongue.

Running his hands firmly up the back of Dalton's thighs, he fingered the crease of the man's ass.

"Oh, love, you're fucking killing me," Dalton said harshly.

Smiling inwardly, Adam continued his torment until Dalton fisted his hair and forced his mouth down over his cock

Adam moaned. Dalton was on the edge of losing control. He would have laughed with glee if he wasn't so turned on. All he could do was groan his approval and encourage Dalton to go for it.

Dalton did just that.

Adam moaned when Dalton took over. It felt like Dalton was bent on tormenting him by pulling his cock out and slapping it at his lips before pushing it back in.

Adam grabbed onto the back of Dalton's legs and chased the tip of Dalton's cock. He needed to feel that cock in his throat, and right now, damn it.

Finally, and with a fisted hand in his hair, Dalton shoved deep inside. Adam gagged but adjusted quickly to the cock that pistoned in and out of his mouth. His own cock dripped with precome and he tugged at himself faster with his free hand while his other traced the line between Dalton's ass cheeks.

The salty taste of Dalton's seed coated his tongue, and Adam made a noise in his throat when a shiver swept down his spine. He shuddered around the cock in his mouth and pulled hard on his own. In a few more seconds, he convulsed, coming on the sweatpants beneath his splayed knees.

His jerking and orgasm sent Dalton over the edge and

the man's grip tightened. With his mouth shoved down on Dalton's cock, the man released.

Adam locked on Dalton's cock when it erupted, coating his tongue and the back of his throat. He swallowed as much as he could and licked up the rest.

Dalton grew still, and the fist in his hair gentled when fingernails caressed his scalp. Adam let the man's limp cock slip from his lips before sitting back on his heels.

He smirked up at the satisfied expression on Dalton's face. Dalton reached down and pulled him up before slipping his fingers within his own and leading him toward the bathroom.

"Mmm an after sex shower."

Dalton snapped on the shower and it heated quickly.

Turning toward him, Dalton eyed his bandage and eased the tape from around the white bandage until his injury was free. The doctor had done a good job and several tiny stitches neatly closed the wound. Dalton bent closer to inspect his knee where he'd slipped outside of Frazer's Gas.

"I'm fine," he said before slipping beneath the warm water. He tipped his head back to let the stream wet his hair.

"I love shower sex," Dalton rumbled, sliding in behind him.

Adam laughed huskily and turned to face the man. "You're insatiable."

"I am."

Adam blinked his eyes open beneath the warm water and grinned. "I need recuperation time."

Dalton smirked and dropped a kiss on his lips. "I didn't mean right now."

"Later though, yes?" Dalton's smirk grew into a smile that warmed the man's eyes.

"Definitely later."

Adam smiled and lifted his mouth to return the kiss beneath the warming spray. Dalton grabbed the soap and ran it over Adam's shoulders and gently down his abs, before reaching his legs.

He balanced with a hand on Dalton's shoulders, his fingers tracing the intricate tattoos. The designs ranged from a pirate wearing a black hat on Dalton's right pec to a Superman symbol on his left shoulder, and everything in between. When Dalton rose upright, Adam caressed his favorite ink. The one that matched his own save for the name difference. They'd gotten the matching heart tattoos when they had been dating. He'd had his redone over the years to keep the red fresh, but it looked as if Dalton had left his alone.

In the center of the heart was Adam's own name etched over Dalton's left pec. The faded red heart also had a lover's arrow through the center.

Lovestruck. The arrow through the heart meant they'd been lovestruck.

"You kept it." He spoke the words he'd wanted to speak while they made love, but he hadn't wanted to break their heated connection.

"You too." Dalton traced his fingers over the tattoo etched over his heart. "It looks new."

"I had the color refreshed."

"What did your fiancé think of that?" One of Dalton's eyebrows lifted.

"He hated it."

"And you didn't think of removing it?"

"It's still here and he isn't."

"Good point."

"Mhmm."

Adam smiled and snatched up the soap. "My turn."

Dalton's breath hissed when he went straight to the man's groin and began washing his sensitive cock and balls.

"Oh," he gazed up from beneath his lashes. "Do you want to wash it?"

Dalton choked out a cough.

"By all means, have at it."

CHAPTER TWENTY-TWO

Dalton

He loved the teasing side of Adam and began to loathe the thought of leaving.

The plan was to arrive back at his parents' house for an early Christmas dinner. Of course, when he'd called his mom and updated her on the time frame, she'd chewed his ear off. He'd appeased her by saying he needed more alone time with Adam. It worked, and she had gushed at the thought of them being back together.

He'd need to leave again once Adam was at his parents' home, but he hoped to God Adam wouldn't disappear. But if he did? Dalton would track him down. Once this whole mess with Sphinx was finished, he was giving Adam his complete focus. The thought made him smile.

Christmas music filled the house with "Santa Claus is Coming to Town." Adam and his holiday music was very cute. If the music wasn't going, then Adam would have a holiday movie going on the TV.

His man was a romantic. His man?

"Here."

Turning from his thoughts and the snow-packed scene out the beach house's front window, he took a hot mug from Adam.

"What is it?" He eyed the dark brown substance that didn't look like coffee.

"It's hot cocoa." Adam huffed out a laugh and dropped a handful of tiny marshmallows in the liquid. Each little white orb bobbed.

Taking a seat on the couch, Adam sat with his back to the corner, sitting crisscross so he had a full view of the room, front door, and window. It wasn't the first time he'd noticed Adam's vigilance. The man was super cautious, double-checking doors and windows every night and morning. When Dalton had asked him about it, Adam's response was that everyone locked their doors at night.

There was locking up and then there was locking down, and Adam was super diligent. Almost as if something had happened to him to make him wary. Dalton rubbed at his chest.

"You're not going to tell me what you did after the Army?" He took a seat on the couch, close enough for his thigh to nudge Adam's toes.

"Odd jobs. I did real estate for a while."

"You sold homes?"

Adam squinted and licked a smudge of cocoa from his upper lip. "Yes, I sold homes. It's an honest living."

"If you say so."

"What does that mean?"

"I don't remember seeing your face on any signs scattered around."

"Scattered around where?" Adam frowned.

"California."

Adam's eyes flew wide. "How'd you know I was in California?"

Dalton smirked and sipped at his own hot chocolate. It was sweet and it tasted damned good. He stayed silent as realization dawned on Adam's face.

"You searched for me."

"I did."

"How long ago."

"After Randy's funeral."

"I wish you would have said hello."

"I wanted to. I drove by your condo once."

"That wasn't my condo. It was Michael's, and I moved out two months after Randy's funeral."

"Then I missed you by a month."

"Fate."

"No," he growled. "It was a missed opportunity. I didn't know you'd broken up with your boyfriend."

"Not a very good spy, are you?"

"Spy?" He snorted. "I could never make a good spy. I'm too straightforward."

"Honest as the day is long," Adam murmured. "Except when it mattered."

Dalton frowned, nodded, and tucked his face into his mug.

Adam sighed. "I'm sorry. I guess I keep bringing it up because… well, you shattered us."

He closed his eyes against the sting, holding back words of sorry. How many times could a man say he was sorry?

Adam needed to figure out if he could forgive him or not. Dalton couldn't help him with that.

The sound of Adam's mug clicked on the glass table next to the couch and in the next moment, the man's fingers were stroking through his hair. Adam scooted closer and placed his head against Dalton's. They sat like that for a long time.

"We can't fall in love."

He closed his eyes. "Too late."

Adam took his cocoa from his hands and placed it aside. Tugging and pulling at him, Adam had him reclining on the couch before stretching out above him.

Now, this was something he could get behind. They'd always burned up the sheets. He sent his hips grinding upward and cupped Adam's tight ass.

"Insatiable," Adam murmured, setting his chin on folded arms against Dalton's chest.

"Only with you."

Adam smiled. "After real estate, of which I washed out by the way... so yeah, no signs with my face on them, I did some technical work for a firm."

"What kind of technical work?"

"They hired me to break into clients' offices."

"What?" Dalton frowned. "For...?"

"To see if the client's security system was up to standards."

"What's the job title for that?"

Adam laughed. "You so want to call me a thief, don't you?"

Dalton let his grin speak for itself.

Adam smacked him on his chest. "I was a consultant. That was my title."

"Was it fun?" It sounded like a blast.

"Yeah, it was fucking fantastic." Adam laughed and

launched into a lively story of breaking in and catching the owner screwing his assistant on his desk.

"Let's just say, I've never seen anyone get dressed so quickly."

"Did he complain?"

"No, he couldn't. He was the one that had hired my firm."

"Maybe he wanted to get caught." Dalton laughed. "Spice things up."

Adam snickered. "My thoughts exactly. So, what about you?"

He had nothing to hide, and he launched into stories of his mercenary days after the Marines and of ending up as second-in-command to a small group of men who helped out people.

"Help out people? What does that mean?" A furrow etched between Adam's eyes.

"Let's just put it this way, when a particular person from Washington calls, we help out. I can't really say more than that." Pegasus was an off-the-books team. Only a handful of people and some local law enforcement knew of their existence.

"You want a house, kids, and picket fence with me, but you can't tell me who you work for?"

"It's not like that." He tightened his hands on Adam's hips when the man tried to pull away. "Promise me forever and I'll tell you everything."

"Blackmail?" Adam looked disappointed in him. "What do you think I'm going to do with the information if we don't work out?" the man said impatiently. "Put it on a billboard sign?"

"No!"

"Then what?"

"I guess keeping the team secret has been ingrained in me," he admitted and stroked his palms over Adam's ass when the man stopped struggling.

"You don't need to keep secrets from me."

"Adam?" He held the man's eyes.

"Yeah?"

"Why do you carry a weapon?"

Silence greeted his question and Adam turned his head, eyes away, cheek resting on his forearms.

It seemed they were at an impasse.

In the end, though, he gave Adam the address to the brewery. Trust had to start with one of them.

"Just in case you ever need me." Saying the words made his chest tighten because it brought up an image of them not together.

Adam smiled and leaned up, kissing his lips, and Dalton pushed his fear aside.

Right here and right now was all that mattered.

CHAPTER TWENTY-THREE

Adam

T**HE REAL ESTATE AND CONSULTANT JOBS HAD ALL BEEN HIS** CIA **cover.**

Everything inside of him wanted to share and open up to Dalton, but he didn't want the light of love disappearing just yet.

Maybe someday he'd tell Dalton.

Maybe.

A shadow near the window sent him rolling out of Dalton's arms and to the floor. Once there, he ran hunched over toward the wall beneath the window.

Dalton was on his feet in seconds.

"Get down," Adam hissed.

Dalton stooped and opened a drawer in the table next to the armchair, pulling out a nine-millimeter handgun.

Chambering a clip, Dalton moved to the side of the window and gazed through the edge of the curtain.

"What did you see?" Dalton asked.

"A shadow of a man."

"Could be Basil," Dalton murmured.

"I didn't hear a car, and why isn't he knocking?"

Boots made a thudding sound on the front porch and Adam regretted keeping his gun tucked away in the spare bedroom. He felt naked without a weapon. Damn it, he was getting lax and soft.

Dalton gave a sudden huff that sounded like a laugh.

"What?"

"It's Gage."

"Gage?" he echoed.

"One of the men from my team."

"Your secret team?" he teased, trying to keep hidden the fact that he was silently poised to run. If this Gage guy suspected that he was Sphinx, he might spill that information to Dalton. Or worse, try to kill him. He'd hate to take out one of Dalton's teammates, but he'd do it if the guy came at him.

"Yeah, the one I gave you the address to." Dalton smirked and held a hand out. Adam took it, letting the man pull him to his feet.

"Come meet Gage."

"I don't want to meet him." Adam tugged at the fingers entwining through his.

Dalton wasn't taking no for an answer and tugged him along to the door. He could have broken away, but that would have meant a tussle with Dalton, and he didn't want to actually hurt the guy.

After bundling up in snow gear, he followed an equally bundled Dalton out onto the front porch.

A man stepped out from the shadows that filled the side of the large porch.

Holy fuck. Gage was huge, menacing, and really sexy. Not as hot as Dalton, but hot damn.

"What are you doing here?" Dalton drawled.

"Tracked your phone. You weren't answering," Gage said.

"I'm on vacation."

"Ace said you were shot at."

"I was, but it's all good now."

"I'll stick around," Gage said.

"Why don't you go into town and get a place. It'll be more comfortable," Dalton suggested, and Adam covered his mouth with his hand to hide his smile.

Talk about subtle...not.

Gage smirked. "I'll check in on Basil."

"Do that," Dalton ordered.

"Answer your phone," Gage growled.

"No. I'll take calls when Christmas is over, not a minute before." He'd been forced to take a vacation, now he only wanted to be left alone with Adam. "Text me if you need me."

Gage raked a glittering gaze over Adam, moving from his face and down his body and back up.

"Got it," the operative said, his voice sounding smug before making his way back through the trees.

He wondered where Gage had parked. Surely the guy hadn't walked in? He looked geared up enough but it was freezing outside.

"We should have offered him some hot cocoa."

"No."

"I thought he was your friend."

Dalton pulled him back into the warmth of the house.

"He is, but he wasn't here in a friend capacity. He has a job to do."

"What is his job?" The guy was big enough to stop a tank. "Enforcer?" Adam joked.

Dalton shucked off his snow jacket and boots and Adam followed suit.

"That and to keep me safe."

"From?"

"A very bad man."

Him... it was him; he was the very bad man. Adam's mouth grew dry. "How bad is this man?"

"Very," Dalton clipped out and Adam knew it was the end of that conversation. Here was his opportunity—to tell Dalton he wasn't a bad man, that he had it all wrong—but he let the moment slip past.

Snatching the cooling cups of hot cocoa from the table, he made his way into the kitchen and popped the mugs into the microwave. He stared at the slowly spinning plate. In the living room, the grate in front of the fireplace scraped and he could hear the thunk of wood being placed.

Opening up the microwave and lifting the mugs out, he rejoined Dalton on the cozy couch. Warmth billowed into the room and the flicker of the lowly lit flames set up a glow with its light reflecting in the room.

"Is he the only one?" Perhaps there were more of Gage's team out there. Maybe it was time to leave the warmth and safety of the beach house.

"I don't know. They're all supposed to be on vacation."

"Then why is Gage here?"

"He's the only one who doesn't have a family that I know of."

"Poor guy. Didn't one of your team ask him to join them?"

"I don't know. I thought maybe Mason might ask him, but I guess that didn't happen."

"Mason?"

"Yeah, another one of my team."

"Is Mason interested in Gage?"

"I thought so, but I can't get a read on Mason."

He grinned. "That bothers you, doesn't it? Not being able to read people."

Dalton shrugged. "Sometimes." The man shot him a glance.

"Oh no," he said with a smirk. "We are not talking about us. Who else is on your team?"

"You're going to make me talk about them, aren't you?"

"Yup."

Dalton studied him for several long moments and Adam held his breath. Would Dalton share with him about his team?

"Well, there's Eagle and Link," Dalton said softly into the silence.

"Are they a couple?"

"Nah. I thought so for a while, but they're just best friends."

"Maybe they're friends with benefits. Like us."

Dalton squinted at him. "I don't want only friendship with you."

"I know." He patted the man's knee. "Stay focused. Who else is on your team?"

He quietly snickered when Dalton snapped his teeth playfully.

"We have Jacob. He's the office computer genius."

"And is he interested in anyone?"

"I honestly don't know." Dalton finished his cocoa and placed the cup aside before turning to him. "Why the interest in other people's love lives?"

LETHAL

"I'm not!" He so was, but he tried to backtrack. "How long has this Jacob guy been with your team?"

"Oh no, you started this." Dalton's smile grew. "The boss is Ace, and he's single."

He laughed when Dalton turned the conversation right back to love lives.

Adam's eyebrows lifted. "Is everyone in your office single?"

A crease etched between Dalton's brows. "Yeah, I think so."

"Gay?"

"Not all, no. At least, I don't think so. Maybe?"

"Do they know you're gay?"

"Yes."

"So, you have Ace, Gage, Mason, Eagle, Link, Jacob, and you?"

"Beckett and Holden, but they are on leave. We used to have Greene, but he retired. Before Ace, there was Wolf and Caleb, but they were on loan."

"Loan?"

"Mhmm, from a second team we have. Wolf and his husband Caleb came down to help form the unit."

"A second team…" That had to be Phoenix. The team from up north. He knew of them through an interagency operation. Pegasus was new, though; he got that much from Dalton's description of his team.

Dalton nodded, fingering one of the dark hairs that fell over Adam's forehead and then gently pushing it back.

A shiver of awareness swept up his back.

"So, you'll hire more?" He sat his own empty cup aside.

"If we need to." Dalton studied him in silence as if mulling something over in his head.

"What?"

"Are you interested?"

"Interested?" He frowned.

"In joining?"

"What? No!" Him in Pegasus? Shit, damn, fuck. Wasn't that a dream come true?

Why did life keep setting him up only to knock him down?

"Think about it."

"Maybe," he rasped and lunged forward to kiss Dalton on the lips and effectively change the conversation.

But it didn't keep him from thinking about all the missed opportunities being blacklisted continued to cost him.

When he got his hands on the guy who had set him up, he was going to strangle him.

Right now, though, he could think of a much better use of his hands.

Over the course of the next few hours, Dalton turned festive. Not only did he coax him into creating the wreath for the front door, but the man boasted of being a wizard at baking. Or so he said, because Adam hadn't seen any baking until tonight.

"You sure you know what you're doing?" Adam glanced doubtfully at the dough.

"Yup." Dalton slapped more flour on the board and patted the lumps into what was to be cookies.

Adam had to admit they were tasty, even if a bit deformed.

After the gingerbread cookie experiment, they'd ended up back in the living room and he spent the time laughing so much, his cheeks hurt from smiling. They didn't talk about the past.

Instead, Adam focused on the present, and right now, with Dalton.

CHAPTER TWENTY-FOUR

One day later.
Dalton

A DAM WAS A VISION IN BRIGHT RED PAJAMAS AND CURLY DARK HAIR. Sitting in the middle of wrapping paper and his family, Adam was surrounded by presents. The glow on the young man's face set up an ache in his chest. The whole room and its occupants looked like a scene from one of those Hallmark Christmas movies. You know, the ones with the happy endings?

He'd hoped it would be that for them. God, he wanted that so fucking bad, and he'd been pretty sure Adam wanted a future with him until last night.

Adam had insisted they come home early this morning to get home before his family opened Christmas presents. The swirling shadows in the man's eyes when he talked about this being his last Christmas with his family broke Dalton's heart.

"This won't be the last one," Dalton had growled.

Adam nodded, but his eyes had remained sad. "We'll see."

Damn it, he wanted another chance with Adam, but Adam was closing off from him, growing more distant as the hours passed.

Something was holding Adam back and it was driving Dalton nuts. He couldn't get Adam to open up. Oh, sure, they talked about the family and the time they'd served in the military, but Adam had dodged any mention of his current job—one that involved two cell phones and a handgun.

The late afternoon Christmas dinner was a grand affair, and he was pretty sure the amount of turkey he'd consumed would interfere with his ability to walk, but Adam made him take a walk around the mansion's interior.

Adam stopped at one of the window alcoves and sat on the window seat. He eased down next to Adam and wrapped his arms around the man's shoulders. They sat like that until the sun sank beneath the horizon and the house lit up with lights once again. His parents would leave the decorations up through the New Year.

"What now?" he murmured, brushing a kiss against Adam's stubbled jaw.

"I need coffee."

He chuckled and pulled Adam to his feet.

Stopping in the kitchen, his mother poured him a hot cup of coffee. He gave her a grateful smile and sprawled in one of the kitchen chairs, his eyes lingering on Adam now sitting opposite.

His mom placed a cup in front of Adam, just as Mary came bouncing into the clean and tidy kitchen.

"Someone named Gage is at the back door for you, Dalton." Mary clutched at her chest. "And oh, my gawd is he HAF!"

"HAF?" Leslie echoed.

"Hush it, he's gay." Dalton gave his sister a stern look and headed to the coffee maker.

"Dang it! All the cute ones are!" Mary said with a pout.

Dalton poured fresh brew in a clean mug and headed toward the back door.

Adam shoved his chair back with a laugh and followed him to the door.

"Why is Gage here?"

"Probably just checking in." Dalton pulled his weapon from the back of his jeans. Vacation or no, the handgun always stayed tucked beneath his loose shirt. "I still haven't turned on my cell phone."

"Tsk, tsk," Adam scolded.

At the back door, Dalton shoved his socked feet into snow boots and pulled on his heavy coat. He waited for Adam to do the same, but Adam shook his head.

"Not coming?"

"Nope, that's your team," Adam said.

Dalton grabbed the man's hand before he could take the stairs that led up to the bedrooms.

"Kiss me."

Adam's brow arched and amusement swam in his pretty blue eyes.

"I kissed you earlier."

"I want another."

"Needy much?"

"Always," he muttered and yanked Adam closer, careful to keep the hot mug of coffee away. Dipping his head, he kissed the man's waiting lips. Adam's tongue swept out and Dalton met it with his own. The taste of coffee lingered, but the rest was all Adam, a flavor he was addicted to.

"I'll be right back."

Stepping outside, Dalton snapped the door closed.

Gage stood just out of the porch light as if to keep his presence hidden. He could have told the guy it was too late, his being there would be all over the house by now. Mary had a panache for gossiping.

"Evening," Gage said.

"Merry Christmas." Dalton approached, handing the hot mug of coffee to Gage.

Gage eyed the weapon in his hand and took the mug.

"Thanks." Gage took a long slow sip and gave what sounded like a grateful sigh.

"Aren't you cold?" He eyed Gage's gloveless hands.

Gage shrugged and motioned toward the street outside of the gates. "It was a short walk from the Jeep."

Dalton had to wonder how Gage had gotten onto the property and made a mental note to speak with the guards at the gates.

A black form moved just outside of Dalton's vision and he pointed his weapon into the murky darkness.

Gage pulled his weapon with his free hand and spun, but the coffee mug Gage held made him a few seconds slower.

"Come out," Dalton snarled through his teeth.

"Hold up," Gage said and lowered his gun. "That's Hunter."

"Hunter? Who the fuck is Hunter?"

"Hunter is a local. Here as a favor to Ace, temporarily filling in while the team is on vacation. I sent him to check on Basil while I watched your ass." Gage finished the coffee.

"Why didn't Ace tell me?" Dalton squinted into the dark, but the shadow had disappeared. He couldn't get a bead on the form of the man.

"Your phone's still off." Gage reminded him of the reason Gage was in Alaska in the first place.

"Hey, Hoss, you'll need to be much quicker than that to get a shot off at me." The back of something hard nudged at his head.

Fuck.

Dalton lowered his gun and sent Gage a scalding glare.

"Knock it off, Hunter. Dalton is the boss."

The man behind him grunted and the hard object was removed. Dalton swung around and swiped his feet out. The asshole was going down. His legs met air. The fucker was fast.

And fucking quick. Hunter had leaped with startling speed.

"Like I said. You'll need to be quicker, *Boss*." Hunter waved the cell phone in his hand at him.

The hard object at the back of his head had been a fucking cell phone, not a gun.

Hunter stepped into the light and Dalton accessed the guy. While Gage's gear wasn't up to par with the current climate, Hunter was loaded for bear. The guy wore cold weather camouflage snow gear and carried an M14 strapped over his shoulder. Even with the military-grade rifle, Hunter had been that quick. Tugging off the black beanie that covered his head, mouth, and face, Hunter shook out his dark hair. Because it was dark, he couldn't see what color the man's eyes were, but they glittered intensely in the Christmas lights. He was attractive, if a person went for the big muscle-bound type.

"You've got a pest problem," Hunter drawled and pointed his rifle toward the street. "Tracks outside go along the side of your property wall."

His heart lurched.

"They didn't get through the gate." Hunter's words stopped him from returning to the house.

"Do I need to worry about how you two got through the gate?" He eyed both men.

"No," Gage drawled.

Hunter smirked. "Whoever those tracks belong to was out there long enough to smoke two cigarettes."

"Get the butts?" He may be able to get a hit on any DNA.

"They left only ashes."

Dalton eyed Hunter. Telling how much a person smoked by only ashes left behind was…well, it was fucking impressive.

"How the hell did they find us?"

Hunter's lips pressed flat and his eyes suddenly turned deadly. "They roughed up the doc."

"Basil? Fuck! Is he okay?" Dalton pulled a hand over his mouth and chin.

"They broke his fucking hand," Hunter hissed.

"Ah, fuck." A surgeon would need his hand. Fucking hell.

"Whoever is after him—" Hunter pointed toward the house, "—isn't going to stop."

It took him a moment to comprehend. "Who, Adam?"

"Yup," Hunter drawled.

"It's not Adam they're after," he corrected the new guy.

"Could have fooled me," Hunter responded flatly.

"So, what's the plan?" Gage interrupted. "You staying here any longer?"

"Just until tomorrow. Then I'm taking down Sphinx."

"Who the fuck is Sphinx?" Hunter asked.

Dalton shot Gage a glance. "I thought you said Ace brought him in."

"He did, but it was to help me. I haven't had time to fill him in."

"Why not?"

"Been kind of busy watching the beach house and mansion," Gage grumbled.

"And you didn't see whoever it was that made those tracks?"

Gage frowned. "When you left the beach house this morning, I found tracks and followed them, but it was only a couple who lives nearby. Whoever was casing the mansion was gone by the time I got here."

It wasn't Gage's fault, but Dalton wasn't in any mood to let any of them off easily. He himself should have been walking this property. This was on him, not Gage.

Gage spun on Hunter. "We're after Sphinx, who is wanted for espionage. That's all I can say out here in the open."

"Agreed." Hunter nodded. "What does he have to do with it?" Again, Hunter pointed his rifle at the house.

"Adam? He's not involved," Dalton said impatiently. "He's an innocent bystander."

"Then why were the men who fucked up Basil asking for Adam's location?" Hunter growled right back.

"They were?" Dalton drew back with a frown, his mind racing. "Men?"

"Yes, two of them," Hunter said.

"Did Sphinx get a partner?" Gage asked.

"I don't know, maybe," Dalton said. "And maybe they want Adam to get to me."

"Maybe," Hunter said, but the guy didn't look convinced.

"Under the circumstances, I think it's best you have Adam stay inside," Gage said.

"Good idea," Hunter said. They all knew that the Weber house was a fortress.

"I'll meet you two tomorrow." Dalton went to turn away, but the sound of approaching sirens filled the air.

"Get inside," Gage urged him. "Until we can figure out if they're legit cops or not."

Dalton didn't stay to argue. Someone had shot at Adam at that gas station, and he had no idea where Sphinx was or who was on the right side of the law. Dalton hurried back into the house.

He couldn't wait until morning; he had to leave tonight and take the danger away from his family.

How the hell was he going to explain that to Adam?

CHAPTER TWENTY-FIVE

Adam

ADAM SMILED AT THE CLOSED BACKDOOR.

Dalton appeared okay with his own refusal to go outside and talk to Gage. Which Adam was grateful for. He didn't need Gage suspecting or discovering who he was. The less he was around Dalton's men, the better.

"Find out if he's bi for me!" Mary hissed.

Adam rolled his eyes at her. "What happened to your boyfriend?"

"Oh, we broke up the other day." Mary waved her hand. "Will you?"

"No." He shook his head. "Trust me, if Gage is gay, and I'm pretty sure Dalton said he is, then Gage won't suddenly become bi for you."

"Oh poo," Mary pouted.

"Yeah, sorry, but it doesn't work that way." Adam snorted.

"I thought we had a connection." Her eyes danced with humor.

"What? Did you think when your eyes met that he'd suddenly turn straight for you?" Adam cackled.

"That's not how it works?" Mary laughed, knowing full well that people didn't choose to be gay. They were or they weren't.

His burner phone buzzed, and he pulled it out of the deep pocket in the bright pajamas, already regretting turning the damned thing on that morning. His heart thundered in his ears.

"I've got to take this," he croaked as he went up the stairs.

Mary disappeared back toward the kitchen and the laughter coming from that room almost made him smile, but the text from Black turned his stomach sour.

I'm sending local PD to your location.

Why? His fingers shook as he typed.

It's time to come in.

Did you find out who set me up? Hope blossomed.

Don't make this difficult, Adam, just go with them when they get there.

The weight was like a heavy boulder settled in his chest and he moved robotically. He'd known this day would come, so he shouldn't be this surprised or this devastated.

Fuck, he and Dalton were out of time. He ran to his bedroom and pulled out an empty backpack and a canteen from the closet. Racing into the private bathroom, he filled up the canteen with fresh water.

He wasn't getting caught until he found the person

who'd burned him. Fuck Black. His handler may be giving up, but it wasn't his fucking life at stake.

He only had a few minutes and rushed back into his bedroom to tuck spare clothes into the pack. Hopping on one foot, he shoved into long underwear and pulled on his cold-weather gear.

A few moments later, he heard the faint sound of sirens. Several seconds later, Dalton called his name from down the hallway.

"Adam?"

Adam finished tying his snow boots, the ones that Dalton had insisted he wear when they'd gone outside together. He was glad for the cold weather gear he'd found of Basil's at the beach house.

Dalton stopped in the doorway of the bedroom and looked over his gear.

"What's going on?"

A lump grew in his throat at the confusion in Dalton's voice.

"I've dreamed of this," Adam said with a sad smile.

"Of what?"

"Of you finding me. Of someday being together again, but that's not the reality."

"What is the reality?" Dalton stepped into the room, slowly approaching him.

"I'm a different person now."

"And I love who you are."

Adam could have cried. All his dreams were coming true and it didn't make a bit of difference. He had to leave.

"I'm in love with you, too, but I can't be with you." He choked the words out.

"Why not?" Dalton's hands clenched into fists.

The sirens grew closer and filled the silence.

"Because of that." Adam pointed toward the window and the flashing lights.

Dalton frowned and stalked to the window to ease back the curtain.

"I have men out there. They won't take me," Dalton said before turning around to look at him. Oh, man did Dalton have it all wrong and he'd run out of time to tell him.

Adam pulled the small flash drive from his wallet and slowly placed it on top of the dresser. Dalton's eyes carefully followed every move he made.

"Don't let that get into the wrong hands," he told Dalton and eased toward the open bathroom door.

Dalton stalked to the dresser and snatched up the flash drive.

"What is it?"

Adam backed closer to the bathroom. "It's important."

Maybe, just maybe, Dalton could get to the bottom of it all. He had to trust Dalton was the man he thought him to be and would know who to take that information to.

As for him? He had to disappear or he really would be a dead man because he was damned sure the sirens were coming to kill him, not arrest Dalton.

"I've got to leave," he said, easing the nine-millimeter from his jacket.

"What? No." Dalton squeezed the flash drive, eyeing the gun.

"Don't come any closer and don't try to stop me." He backed toward the bathroom door.

"Adam, what the hell is going on?"

His next words stopped Dalton in his tracks.

"I wish we had more time. I wish things were

different. Please know that." Tears stung his eyes and he didn't try to hold them back.

Fuck it. He'd cried over Dalton plenty, what were a few more tears?

"I love you. Remember that," he croaked and sprinted into the bathroom and slammed the door. The door snapped into place, and he wedged the wrought iron vanity chair beneath the knob.

"Adam!" Dalton tried the knob and then slammed a shoulder into the heavy, hard oak. The vanity chair's legs slid and then caught and held.

The door would eventually crack beneath the force of Dalton's strength and the chair would topple, but it would give him enough time to get gone.

Adam raced to the bathroom window that he had previously made sure would open easily. It lifted beneath his hands. He was outside in a flash, his snow boots digging in deep with the cleats on the bottoms. He scrambled down the roof, his boots keeping him from slipping. The darkness closed in around him as he hit the trellis that ran up the side of the house. He swung himself down and was running when he hit the ground. Moving into the trees of the property, he tossed the rope he'd found earlier in the garage over the wall. In seconds, he was up and over. He only stopped to breathe when the Alaska wilderness closed in around him.

The sirens faded as he moved farther away from the mansion. At one point, he paused, sure that someone was following him, but when he stopped, the noise stopped.

The silence of the forest rang, broken only by the fall of snow slipping from piled high branches. Even the sirens had stopped.

He had no plans to linger here. Fairbanks was a few

miles away. He could disappear in a big city that size. There was a bus terminal where he could take a ride south. Hell, he'd hitchhike if he had to.

A crunch sounded and he dropped low and stilled. Whoever the fuck was following him was fucking good.

But he was better.

He had to be.

His life depended on escape.

CHAPTER TWENTY-SIX

Dalton

THE KITCHEN CHAIR FELT HARD BENEATH HIS ASS.

The men across from him wore equally hard faces.

"Did you know that your friend, Adam Campbell, was Sphinx?"

"No," he said for the fiftieth time.

"Did he say anything about his plans with the list?"

"No," he responded evenly, his hand hidden in his pocket squeezed around the flash drive.

He only had to stall until his men arrived.

Gage had gone for help.

Hunter was... fuck knew where.

And Adam?

Adam was Sphinx.

It all made sense now, his crazy attraction to Sphinx plus all of Adam's secrecy. He should have known. He felt numb—still finding it hard to wrap his head around the fact that Adam was the criminal he'd been hunting all this time.

Adam had lied to him.

No, he hadn't. He just didn't tell him who he was.

Yes, he did, he silently corrected.

"I work for a top-secret organization! I can't tell you which one or I'd have to kill you."

Adam's earlier words came back to haunt him. Adam did warn him that he wasn't the man he thought him to be.

Fuck.

Dalton felt all kinds of stupid.

And rage. His hands curled into fists at being duped. But had he been duped? He knew Adam felt something for him. For fuck's sake, Adam loved him. Those had been real tears.

Tears filled with regret.

"Are you listening?"

Dalton leveled his eyes on the fucker across the table and pictured a bullet hole in the middle of the guy's forehead. If either one of these fuckers were involved with trying to kill Adam, they were dead men.

After one look at the men who came to question her son, Leslie had packed up his dad and siblings and left by way of the family helicopter. They used it in case of emergencies. He wasn't worried about his family—his dad was ex-military and an accomplished pilot. His mom? Well, she was best friends with some pretty powerful people. She'd sent him a text fifteen minutes ago saying they'd all arrived at the governor's home. She'd said she'd sent help.

He'd responded with, "Don't bother yet," before his phone was taken by the clown on his left.

LETHAL

"Answer his fucking question." The agent's tone turned ugly.

"What?" He pinched at the bridge of his nose, trying to remember the question. "I told you, I didn't know Adam is Sphinx. I didn't see any list."

The man who asked most of the questions wiped a rag over his sweating brow. The guy was dripping and that was a fucking tell—he was nervous as hell.

"Who do you work for again?" Dalton asked. When they glared at him, he smirked.

"The FBI," the sweating agent said.

"Are you sure those are real badges?" Dalton nodded to the coat pockets that both suits wore.

Boots stomped on the porch and then the door opened.

The two agents shoved to their feet, but it was too late.

Mason, with his blond hair all askew, stepped inside. The operative held two handguns with arms outstretched. Mason trained a gun on each of the agents.

"No, no, no," Mason cautioned when one of the guys moved to pull a weapon.

"You're in a world of shit for pointing that gun at us," the ugly-toned agent growled.

"I'll tell that to my therapist." Mason waved a gun at one of them. "Now, with two fingers, take out your weapons and lay them on the floor."

Dalton didn't move until the agents complied with Mason's demand and were reseated.

"What the hell are you doing here?" He stood and grabbed up his phone.

"You didn't think I'd let Gage come alone, did you?"

"What about the family?"

"It's all good." Mason gave a smirk.

"Well then, what took you so long?" He scowled.

Adam had a two-hour head start, there was no telling where he was now.

"I wasn't standing outside your house waiting," Mason said with a snort. "Gage drove me in from town."

Gage's big form suddenly filled the open doorway. The man's scowl was a thunderstorm and aimed at Mason.

"What?" Mason asked innocently of Gage. "Did you want me to wait while you parked the car?"

"I asked you to," Gage growled and zip-tied the agent's hands together and then to the front of the kitchen stove.

"I can't help it if I'm faster than you," Mason said with a shrug.

Gage's nostrils flared and Dalton stepped in before the pair could exchange blows.

"What's the extraction plan?" he snapped, moving toward the door.

"You can't leave us here like this!" one agent shouted.

"The hell I can't." Mason laughed and closed the door once Gage was outside.

"Ace sent a chopper. It's in the ballfield near town," Gage said, heading to a black SUV parked in the driveway.

"Why didn't he just use our landing pad?" Dalton asked as he slid into the back seat.

"Maybe he thought it was occupied?" Gage jumped into the passenger side.

Mason, behind the wheel, slammed on the gas and roared down the road.

Dalton would send a text to his brother that it was safe to come home, but only after the agents were out of there.

He had to wonder how much trouble they'd be in for accosting federal agents.

"Where's your phone?" Gage glanced over his shoulder at him from the passenger seat.

Dalton pulled his cell from his pocket. He'd forgotten to charge it last night and it had died earlier after sending the text to his mother.

"It's dead."

"You didn't charge your phone?" Gage sounded incredulous.

"It's Christmas," he growled. Sue him, he hadn't thought about charging the fucking thing.

It was Adam. Adam made him forget where he was and the job he was supposed to be doing.

Mason punched the button on the steering wheel and a few seconds later, the ringing of a phone filled the speakers.

"Tell me you fucking have Dalton," Ace snarled.

"Yeah, they have me," he said.

"Fuck!" The word was filled with relief and anger. "What the fuck is going on?"

"I'll tell you what I know." He swallowed. "Adam is Sphinx."

"Shit," Ace said.

That was an understatement.

Gage and Mason exchanged looks. They hadn't been there when the agents questioned him.

"There's more."

"What?"

"Adam... Sphinx gave me a flash drive."

"With the list?" Ace asked sharply.

"I think so," he said, because he didn't know.

"Get back here ASAP."

"On it."

Gage grabbed the "oh shit" handle when Mason punched the gas, sending the tires spinning in the snow.

"In one piece!" Gage growled.

Mason laughed, and it sounded a bit diabolical.

Dalton gazed out the window at the dark landscape and wondered if Adam was safe.

Of course, he was safe.

He was Sphinx.

• • •

Sitting in Ace's office the next morning, Dalton was still trying to wrap his head around the fact that Adam was indeed the criminal he'd been hunting.

"Dave, are you ready?" Ace glanced at the wall monitor and the SecDef sitting behind a desk at an undisclosed location. Ace used a virtual conference platform in order for the unit to view the meeting with the SecDef.

"As ready as I'll ever be." Dave gave them a nod.

"Okay, here we go." Ace inserted the flash drive into the laptop and Dave's office disappeared from the wall monitor.

Adam's face filled the screen.

"If you're watching this, then I'm probably dead."

His breath caught and his chest squeezed. No way in hell was Adam dead. He'd feel it. He'd know it.

"He's not dead," he said, his voice harsh in the room.

Nobody spoke.

Adam continued. "If that is the case, then I want my story to get out. I want the truth of what happened to be told, and I hope whoever is watching this will do the right thing."

"Fuck yeah, we'll do the right thing," Eagle growled from the chair at his right. His friend's hand clamped comfortably on Dalton's shoulder.

"My name is Adam Campbell. My code name is Sphinx and I work...worked for the CIA until I was recently burned."

Every pair of eyes were riveted to the screen. Dalton gripped the chair's arms.

"While my normal handler was on leave, I was contacted by an unknown CIA agent. He had all the codes and whatnots to gain my trust. So, I think this was an inside job. I was tasked with gaining possession of a flash drive. I was told it was a list. It was not."

"Not a list?" Mason echoed.

"Hush." Gage gave the guy a stern look. Mason gave Gage the finger.

"What I'm about to show you is the contents of that flash drive."

Adam's face faded from the screen and Dalton missed him immediately.

The scene that unfolded was of a man handing another man a folder. A third man approached and shot the two men and took the folder.

"Fucking hell," Ace muttered, his face—tight and pale—focused on the screen.

Adam's face came back on the screen. "I don't know what was in the folder, but the man you just saw murder two people is—"

"Senator Metzler," the SecDef said, his voice overriding Adam's through the speakers.

Ace stopped the video and both Adam's paused face and Dave's filled the screen.

"What the fuck?" Eagle scowled. It was just like Eagle to not give a flying fuck who he was talking to.

"Keep going," Dave told Ace.

Ace gave a short nod and again started the video.

"I suspect that the person within the CIA who sent me to get the flash drive is being paid by the senator. Or works for him. I don't know. All I do know is that when I looked at the contents of the flash drive, my house was seized, my bank accounts were frozen, and I became a wanted fugitive. It didn't dawn on me until after looking at the contents of the incriminating video that I was being used as a pawn to retrieve the drive from a person blackmailing the senator."

Adam went on to tell them the name of the blackmailer.

"One more thing," Adam said after a moment. "I was assured my CIA handler Richard Black would help clear my name, yet all Black seems to want is this flash drive, and I can't figure out if he's involved or not." Adam rubbed at his mouth. Worry etched across his handsome face. "Black sent me into the city last night to meet an informant." Adam glanced at his watch. "As I'm recording this, it's December 21st. All I know is that the informant didn't show up and there was an accident on the road."

Adam must have recorded this video at the beach house. The only time Dalton had left Adam alone had been to get groceries. Adam had offered to stay back and get the decorations ready.

Ace again paused the video.

"The 21st... That's the day after FBI agent Farnsworth was killed," Dalton said.

"Where was Adam the night of Farnsworth's death?"

"He was at Frazer's Gas. I left him there so he could

get cookies." He ignored the strange looks from the team. "That's when I found out that Farnsworth had been run off the road and killed. No way did Adam have enough time to do that."

"Where was Adam when he recorded this?" Ace said.

"He was with me at the beach house. I had slipped out to get groceries," Dalton told Ace.

"Got it," Ace said with a nod and started the recording again.

"The FBI most wanted list has me as a killer," Adam continued. "I didn't kill that FBI agent. Dalton Weber can vouch for me on that. I looked up the time of death. I was at the Weber house."

Several pairs of eyes swiveled to him, but he didn't give a fuck. Of course, he'd vouch for Adam, and he'd already done just that.

"Dalton, if you're watching this and...I am dead, just know that you were the love of my life."

The screen blurred and he thought it was a technical error, but it wasn't. He wiped a hand down his face, taking the tears with it.

"Those motherfuckers are going to pay." He turned his burning gaze to Ace and then Dave. "Every last one of them," he finished through his teeth.

"Agreed," Ace murmured.

The room grew quiet until a commotion outside in the bullpen happened.

"I'll call you back, Dave," Ace said, ending the video conference.

Dalton shoved to his feet at the sound of Jacob's angry voice. The rest of the team was out of their chairs and leaping for the door.

"I don't care, you asshole, stop or I'll put a bullet in your ass."

In the bullpen stood Jacob Burns holding a gun on Hunter.

"Jacob," Ace soothed the agitated young man. "It's okay, Hunter is with us."

Jacob's eyes burned brightly at the massive man standing with his hands up in the air. Hunter had a bemused look on his face. And a cut over his right eye.

"Where the hell have you been?" Dalton growled at Hunter.

"What happened to your face?" Mason asked.

"Lower your hands." Jacob gestured with his gun before tucking it away in the shoulder holster he wore.

"How did you get inside?" Eagle rasped.

"Me." Oliver Rains, former Special Forces soldier from the unit Infinity, stood in the doorway with a raised hand. "Ace gave me the code." Oliver looked guilty.

"Yeah, thanks for the backup," Hunter snapped at Oliver.

"Looked like you were doing just fine." Oliver gave Hunter a quick smile and clapped his hands together. "It was a long drive. Got any food around?"

"Order pizza." Ace closed a hand on Jacob's shoulder and gently turned the younger man toward the communications room. "Please."

After a hard stare at Hunter, Jacob held Ace's gaze for a quick moment.

"Pepperoni?" Jacob asked Ace.

One corner of Ace's mouth tipped. "Is there any other kind?"

"Well, yeah." Jacob gave a quick smile, dimples flashing, and disappeared.

Ace spun on Hunter; it was a move so powerful, Hunter actually took a step back. "I don't know what you did to piss Jacob off, but you better fix it," their commander growled.

"I will," Hunter said on a swallow and glanced away.

"Now, answer Mason's question," Ace said. "What happened to your face?"

Hunter turned on Dalton with a frown.

"Sphinx did this when I caught up with him in Phoenix." Hunter pointed to the cut over one eye.

Dalton smirked and then grinned with a huge wave of relief. Sphinx had gotten the drop on Hunter. It was justice at its finest since in Alaska, Hunter had gotten the drop on Dalton.

Sphinx was that good, but more importantly…

Adam was alive.

CHAPTER TWENTY-SEVEN

Adam

H E'D THROWN OFF HIS TAIL SOMEWHERE IN PHOENIX.
The poor sap hadn't stood a chance against his skills. He had to hand it to the guy, though, it hadn't been easy. In fact, it had been damned difficult, but not as difficult as what he was about to attempt next.

Dialing his handler's number, he waited for the man to pick up.

"Adam?"

"What's going on?" he said. "Are you in on it? Did you take money?"

Richard Black's heavy sigh came over the line. "You always were too smart for your own good. You should have just walked away."

Bile rose in his throat. Easing to the window, Adam glanced through the slit between the curtains of the dirty roadside motel somewhere near the border of Pasadena, California. The street sat dark and dingy beyond the heavy curtain except for a few street workers and the homeless. The outside parking lot of the motel was dark, dismal, and more importantly, empty. That didn't mean they weren't out there waiting to kill him.

"Call off your dogs."

"I would if they were my dogs."

Black may be trying to blame the senator, but the senator had to have had help to pull off blacklisting him. Had Black used a voice changer when he had given him the orders to steal the flash drive?

"I know about the senator. How long have you been in his pocket?"

An annoyed-sounding sigh came over the line, but Adam didn't give a fuck. He was going to get answers, one way or another.

"What I can't figure out is why Charlotte Mills would film him," he went on with a soft murmur, watching a homeless woman push a shopping cart down the sidewalk across the wet street.

Black stayed silent.

"You might as well tell me. I know everything else."

"I'm a dead man if I do."

"You're a dead man anyway when I find you." He needed to make that very clear to Black. He wouldn't leave Black alive to do this to anyone else.

"You'd do that?" Black asked, sounding surprised.

"Seriously? The guy who is trying to kill me is asking if I'd shoot him dead," Adam sneered. "Talk about fucking ironic."

There was another long moment of silence before Black finally spoke.

"Charlotte Mills was blackmailing the senator."

"What the hell for?"

"Money."

"Obviously," he snapped. "What did she have on him?"

"Charlotte had proof of his affair with a call girl and threatened to go to his wife. She set up a meeting to hand the pictures over for a lump sum. When the senator arrived, he shot both people and took the photos."

"So, she was the one filming the shooting from afar. Smart girl," Adam said. "Who were the people the senator killed?"

"Friends of Charlotte Mills."

"Where is she?"

"She's dead."

"You assholes. Why me?"

"Because of your skills with breaking and entering. You see, Charlotte stashed the flash drive in a state-of-the-art facility. You were the best choice for the job."

"Thanks. Not," he muttered.

"You're the only loose end," Black continued.

"I'm the thorn in the senator's side? Well, doesn't that gladden my heart." He gave a bitter laugh. "Did the senator have her killed?"

"She didn't suffer." The tone in Black's voice spoke volumes.

"You fuckers will stop at nothing to keep a dirty politician hidden," he said with a sneer.

"Where are you?" Black said.

Adam glanced back through the slit between the curtains when a vehicle approached. A beat-up old pickup pulled into the hotel parking lot and a family of four jumped out. Other than that, the area remained empty.

"Somewhere in Pasadena, California," he murmured. It

wasn't quite the same city, but it was close enough to Ventura for his plan to work.

"Right," Black said with a disbelieving tone.

"Don't believe me?"

"The chances of you telling me the truth are slim."

"And who's to blame for that?" Adam rubbed at the hair growing along his upper lip. "I trusted you."

"I'm sorry," Black said, sounding anything but.

"No, you're not. You don't regret a fucking thing."

The silence rang over the phone. Black didn't respond.

"Black?"

"Yeah?"

"But you will be."

"Will be what?"

"Sorry." Adam pushed the end button and tucked the burner into his pocket.

He made sure to leave the phone turned on. If they couldn't trace him, then they couldn't find him, and he needed to be found to make his plan work.

The hands on his watch showed just after four-thirty in the evening. He wondered if he was too late and the team would have gone home.

Oh well, better late than never, right?

• • •

Roughly an hour and ten minutes later, Adam stood on the sidewalk looking at the flashing neon sign over a dark brown building in the busy district of the city of Ventura. People walked around him—couples and groups wandering their way through the damp Friday evening. Some would enter the establishment and others would walk on past, window shopping.

A large muscled man stood at the door carding entry, which would have been strange if he didn't already know what kind of place this really was.

"Of all the stupid things to do," he muttered under his breath and approached the guy at the door.

"I thought you were going to stand outside all night," the big bouncer wearing a tight t-shirt and new looking jeans said with a smile.

Okay, carding people at a brewery and a very observant bouncer. Figures.

"Nah, was just working up the nerve," he murmured and handed the man his real ID.

"We don't bite." The man with the name Peter sewn with white thread in small letters on the breast of the black t-shirt gave him a flirty smile. "At least, not hard." Peter's eyes lifted from his license. "Have fun, Adam Campbell."

There was zero recognition of his name flickering in the man's eyes. Okay, so far, so good.

"Thanks." Adam slipped his ID away and stepped through the door.

The noise was instant. The smell of a toasty, malty aroma drifted in the air along with deep-fried food and popcorn. Laughter, music, and conversations assaulted his eardrums. He was scoped out immediately by men dressed similar to Peter—two men near the door and the bartender behind the bar. A couple crowded in behind him and Adam stepped farther into the bodies surrounding the bar before he stopped.

"First time here?" the man behind him said when he hesitated.

"Yeah." He turned and smiled at the older couple.

"Come on," the woman said with a friendly smile. "We have a table reserved."

Adam shook his head. "I don't want to impose."

"You won't be," the man insisted. "And my wife won't take no for an answer."

Giving in with a smile, Adam followed the husband and wife duo to a high table near the back. It was perfect, really. He couldn't have planned it better.

"How do you have a table reserved?" Adam asked.

"Our son works here," the woman gushed as her husband helped her off with her coat and gave their order to one of the servers milling about.

Adam glanced over the room. Yep. This wasn't your regular old run-of-the-mill brewery. For one, Pegasus sat somewhere below and for another, it was livelier than any brewery he'd ever been inside. A guitarist played a happy tune while the drummer and singer harmonized. In front of the small stage lay a dance floor, packed with couples. Mostly gay and lesbian couples and a few odd straight ones.

The place held a mix of customers that screamed inclusivity, and he fucking loved it.

CHAPTER TWENTY-EIGHT

Dalton

THE INTERCOM BUZZED AT ACE'S DESK.

"What's up, Peter?" Ace asked the front doorman.

"Adam Campbell has entered the building."

The words stopped Dalton cold...for two seconds...and then he launched to the panel of monitors near the far wall of the bullpen. He slapped a button and the wall lit up with video footage of the brewery upstairs.

The rest of the team had shoved up from various places and came closer.

Dalton ignored them all, his eyes combing over every single person.

"There." Hunter pointed to the left bottom screen and Dalton's eyes shot to that monitor.

Sure enough, Adam stood talking to Cooper's parents

at a table near the wall. It wasn't too close to the exit, but it was close enough.

"Tell Peter to watch the exit, but under no circumstances is he to get in Adam's way if he tries to leave."

"Are you serious?" Hunter growled.

"Back the fuck down," Dalton snarled, turning on the new guy. "We want him alive, not dead. If that means tailing him, then that's what we'll do."

"Sorry." Hunter shifted beneath his penetrating stare.

Dalton turned his back on the guy and snatched his nine-millimeter from the desk and slipped it into his shoulder holster.

"What's the plan?" Ace asked from where he leaned against the door jamb of his office.

"I'm going up there to talk with him."

"You aren't going alone," Eagle said. His friend may have sounded conversational, but he heard the intent beneath the words. Eagle wasn't letting him go without backup.

"Adam won't hurt me. He might kill one of you though." Dalton squinted at Eagle.

Eagle smiled—a *bring it, motherfucker* type of smile. "He can try."

Dalton closed his eyes in exasperation.

"If you think I'm staying back, you're dead wrong," Gage's deep voice boomed.

"Where he goes, I go," Mason piped up.

Gage's eyes snapped to Mason. "Really?"

"No." Mason's lips pressed flat.

"Ass." Gage's nostrils flared.

"Fucking hell, the last thing I need is you clowns messing this up." Dalton stalked to the door that led to the small set of stairs upward.

"Then let's stop arguing and get up there," Link said.

Dalton moved up the stairs and when he reached the hallway, he glanced back. Gage, Eagle, and Link were behind him. There was no sign of Mason, Ace, or Hunter.

"Spread out when we get up there but under no circumstances are you to approach him," he told the three.

Dalton didn't move until all heads bobbed in acknowledgment.

Gage took a seat at the bar and Eagle and Link made their way casually toward the front exit.

Inside, the bar area was noisy and crowded. Friday and Saturday were the busiest nights for them.

Adam's head popped up as if suddenly noticing him, but Dalton kept his eyes averted and made his way to the bar.

"The usual?" Cooper asked.

"Please. Give me two of them."

Two glasses of cranberry over ice were set before him and he lifted them up and moved smoothly through the crowd. It was easy with his size; people just generally moved aside.

Reaching the high table where Adam stood listening to Mr. and Mrs. Lancaster talk about their trip to Hollywood, Dalton stopped next to Adam.

"Dalton!" Mr. Lancaster offered his hand.

"How was the trip?" He clasped the older man's hand in a gentle but firm grip. Their head bartender's parents had to be pushing eighty but showed no signs of slowing down.

"It was lovely!" Mrs. Lancaster answered. "Thank you for giving Cooper time off to go with us."

Dalton tossed a glance at the bar. Sure enough, Cooper was watching them with a cool, intense gaze.

LETHAL

Cooper was their secret weapon outside of the bullpen. The man had joined Pegasus three months prior as lead bartender and shit-kicker if things got dicey in the brewery. He was the first one who stood in the way of any attack here on their home turf. The ex-Special Forces soldier gave him a slow nod and then barked an order at a fumbling server. When the tray the man held wobbled, Cooper stepped up and relieved the server of the heavy object and then nodded toward the customers. The server led the way to the table and Cooper followed, hefting the heavy tray with ease.

Of course, Cooper's parents knew nothing about the man's real job.

"Is one of those for me?"

Adam's voice brought his eyes back to the man's upturned face. Adam's head tipped slowly to the side just a bit, so much like Sphinx that Dalton wondered how in the hell he hadn't seen the similarity before. Long, thick lashes swept upward, revealing those bright blue eyes. The expression in Adam's eyes was a mix of trepidation and excitement.

Dalton couldn't help but let his lips curl at the corners. Damn it, Adam rang every single bell in his heart, body, and mind.

"Of course." He handed the glass to Adam and dipped his head down.

Adam's breath caught.

Dalton held the man's glittering gaze and then gently brushed a kiss to Adam's cheek. He'd wanted to take Adam's lips, but public displays were not his thing.

"Aww, how cute!" Mrs. Lancaster clapped her hands. "Is this your man, Dalton?"

"Yes," he answered her before Adam could say differently.

The humor in Adam's gaze grew. Lifting the glass to his lips, Adam swallowed down every bit of the cranberry before setting the glass aside, his tongue darting out to lick at his lips.

Dalton almost choked on his own drink at the little teasing move but managed to drain his glass.

"Can you excuse us?" Dalton said to the couple and placed his empty glass aside. Setting his free hand on Adam's back, he eased his palm lower, near the man's hips.

"Oh sure!" Mr. Lancaster said with a smile.

"Where are we going?" Adam glanced up, catching his gaze as they moved toward the door that would take them back down to Pegasus' offices.

"Down."

"Down? Like in a dungeon? Will there be whips and chains?"

Dalton couldn't help his abrupt bark of laughter.

"Don't tempt me," he muttered with a reluctant smile.

"Why not?" Adam said, walking with him through the crowded room.

"We have a lot to discuss."

"Yeah, yeah, but first…" Adam's fingers laced with his and before he could react, Dalton found himself on the dance floor in the midst of dancing bodies.

"No." He stood watching Adam snap his fingers to the beat.

"Dance with me." Adam smiled, lifted his arms, and gyrated his hips.

"No," he growled, his hunger rising.

"Yes." Not taking no for an answer, Adam spun and danced back into him.

Dalton hissed when Adam's ass ground up against his crotch. He placed his hands on Adam's hips and when Adam leaned his back against his chest and ground his ass into his groin, Dalton dipped his head.

Sliding his arms around Adam's waist, he kept the man plastered to his body while his mouth roamed the skin at the side of Adam's neck.

The beat thrummed. Dalton's pulse hammered and the room faded. The only thing on earth that mattered was this man in his arms.

And it didn't make a bit of difference to his heart that Adam was Sphinx.

CHAPTER TWENTY-NINE

Adam

Dalton had a habit of making him feel like the only person on earth.

He spun in Dalton's arms to the music, facing the man, and crowded in closer before slipping his arms up and around Dalton's neck.

"Stay with me," Dalton said in a husky whisper.

"I'm here." But for how much longer, he couldn't be sure. There was so much left to be done.

A commotion at the front door drew his gaze in that direction. People near that half of the room went scrambling. A woman screamed, the sound traveling over the pounding beat of the music.

"Get back!" a booming voice said from near the front door.

It took Adam a second to recognize the man in the

LETHAL

doorway. He was one of the FBI agents sent to kill him. Behind the guy were several armed men, all wearing black, equipped with weapons and no badges showing. Were they hired guns? Just fucking great. He'd expected a force, but not this!

The bouncer, Peter, was trying to contain the situation, but he was no match for the number of armed men pouring in through the door. Peter, as big as he was, went down beneath the crush of men entering.

Dalton tensed and dropped low, dragging him down. People around them started to notice the growing noise. A back door that sat between the end of the bar and the dance floor banged open and several men charged out.

He recognized the one he'd come up against in Phoenix, and a few others that had been outside of the apartment building that cold, dark night.

These were Dalton's men. Every single one of them carried a weapon. Even the guy behind the bar lifted a shotgun and chambered a bullet.

"You with me?" Dalton growled, gaining his attention from the chaos of the room.

"What's the plan?"

"Stay low. I'll get you out of here."

"Not going to have me arrested?"

"Did you think I would?" Dalton frowned and yanked at his hand before he could answer. Running hunched over through the crush of confused people, Dalton headed toward the door by the bar.

Entering through the wood door, Dalton closed it and pulled him down a wide but short hallway to a set of four stairs leading down to a steel door.

They got to the door where Dalton put his face to a small

screen and then used a thumb lock and entered a code. The thick metal door flicked open and Dalton hurried through.

Adam stopped and pulled from Dalton's hand.

"What?" Dalton frowned at him in the doorway.

"I'm not running." He tipped his chin. "I'm going back out there and getting that bastard to tell me what the fuck is going on."

"At least wait until we can contact the SecDef. Those assholes out there have the power to arrest you on the spot," Dalton urged, slow steps bringing him back toward him.

In the next moment, an explosion rocked the building. Adam's eyes flew wide and Dalton's face paled.

"Motherfuckers," Dalton spat and raced to a desk, grabbing extra clips.

Adam pulled his weapon out and aimed it at the hallway they'd come from. The noise beyond the outer door was deafening with gunfire and screaming. The explosion had to have damaged the foundation of the place.

"What the fuck is going on?" A young, dark-haired man came out of an office to his right and Adam had two seconds to take in the guy's worried look before a loud bang sounded on the wooden door down the hall.

"We're outnumbered," Adam hissed.

"Jacob," Dalton growled. "Pull on a vest and call the SecDef. Can you do that? Tell them Ace is in trouble. The Pegasus facility is under attack."

Jacob turned white as a sheet. His blue eyes burned in his face, but the next instant, he yanked a vest off the wall, shoved his arms into it, and raced to an office off the main room.

Adam heard a bullet punch through the wood door and smack into the hallway wall.

"They're breaching," he spat and moved back out the

steel door and to the top of the small set of stairs. Dalton joined him after closing the thick steel door.

"You have a plan?" Adam said when Dalton settled his big body next to him.

"We don't have coms in," Dalton grumbled. "I have no way of knowing what's going on up there. I have to go up."

"You go, I go," he said.

"I know." Dalton gave him a rueful smile and then shoved up and out of the small stairway. Moving in sync back down the short hallway felt like a fucking gauntlet. They were sitting ducks if the wooden door didn't hold. He suspected that the only reason it hadn't opened was Dalton's men standing in Black's way. And even though he hadn't seen Black, he was pretty fucking sure his ex-handler was somewhere out there.

The screaming noises from the other side had subsided and he wondered how many wounded lay out there needing medical help.

"This is my fault. I led them here," he croaked, having no idea how Black could have found him so fast.

"No, you didn't. That lead guy out there is FBI agent Sweenie, and he and his thugs have been here before," Dalton growled.

Relief swept over him, but it didn't make the situation change. They were still outgunned and innocent civilians were involved.

The wood door at the end of the hallway flew open with a loud crack just as the metal one behind them opened.

"Jacob, get back inside and close the door. That's an order," Dalton growled.

"Fuck that," Jacob spat and crouched in the stairwell behind them with a gun in hand. "I contacted the SecDef. He says he's sending help."

"In the form of who?"

"Well, my dads, for one." Jacob gave them a cocky grin.

Before he could ask about the plural "dads" comment, a large man appeared in the doorway. The man was fucked up; blood dripped down the side of his face and he was holding one arm against his chest. Soot and debris littered him, and Adam would bet money the guy had been caught in the blast. He looked like not much past an explosion could take him down. Not that he was huge or anything, it was his eyes. They were piercing and commanding and suddenly filled with horror when they landed on Jacob.

Another man, this one with a gunshot wound, was shoved through.

An agent, and he used the term Agent loosely, was holding a gun to the slighter man's temple.

"Back up or he's dead."

Everyone froze.

Dalton slowly, and out of sight from the group, pushed on Jacob's shoulder, urging him back. Jacob crouched, keeping out of sight.

"I have nothing to lose," the agent spat, grinding the gun into the slighter man's temple.

CHAPTER THIRTY

Dalton

ACE WAS BEING CONTROLLED BY THE GUN PRESSED INTO OLIVER Rain's temple and Dalton had no doubt that Ace would do whatever it took to save one of their own.

Poor Oliver. The man had driven down to scope out the facility with the possibility of joining them.

Welcome to fucking Pegasus.

Dalton waited. Ace returned to holding his eyes after that one shocked look at Jacob. Good thing the bad guys couldn't see Jacob on account the younger man was hunkered down behind Dalton. Only Ace, at his height, had a good view of the small set of stairs.

Dalton reached back and motioned slowly with his hand to Jacob. The younger man slipped back and disappeared into the office without a word.

Dalton lowered his weapon to the floor and Adam

followed suit. He hadn't asked Adam, nor would he ask him to surrender, but Oliver's life was on the line. The Adam he knew would do everything in his power to save a life.

"Now," Agent Sweenie said, using Oliver as a shield along with the gun to the guy's head, "open the fucking door."

Oliver was barely hanging on. It looked like he might have taken part of the blast to one leg, along with the bullet wound in his stomach. Blood soaked the front of his shirt and pants.

Ace hesitated.

"Open it now or he'll be dead like your fucking bartender."

They'd killed Cooper? And Cooper's parents? Had they made it out alive? And where the fuck was the rest of his unit?

"Open it," Ace ordered, and Dalton did as he was told.

Backing up slowly, Dalton pulled Adam with him through the steel door and back into the bullpen.

"Fan out," Sweenie ordered.

Four armed thugs shoved past them and through the bullpen, disappearing into the hallway and offices beyond. Two more perps stayed flanking Sweenie.

Fuck. He hoped Jacob had hidden somewhere and didn't try any cowboy shit.

"You didn't think I could catch you, did you?" Agent Sweenie sneered at Adam as he moved Oliver closer by way of a fist to the back of the man's shirt.

"Let's get one thing clear. I let you catch me, you fuck-wad," Adam said in a tone of voice that sounded almost conversational, calm.

"Sir," one of Sweenie's men said and stepped up to whisper in the guy's ear.

Wait, what? Dalton gazed down at Adam.

Had Adam let himself be caught? It suddenly dawned on

Dalton that Adam might have a backup plan. Thank fucking hell.

"Did you have a plan?" he whispered while Sweenie was distracted.

"Um, yeah. You guys were my plan," Adam whispered back.

Well just fucking great.

"All right, time's up," Sweenie said after two of his men disappeared back out the steel door. "What's it going to be, Sphinx?"

"I'll go," Adam said.

"No," Dalton growled, his stomach souring.

"It's my choice," Adam reminded him and turned back to Sweenie. "I'll go if you leave him alone." Adam gestured to Oliver.

Sweenie jerked his head at the remaining man to his left. The guy stepped up and put his gun to Oliver's head. Oliver's eyes burned in his face and Dalton knew the ex-Special Forces soldier would have gone ballistic if not for his injuries. Blood pooled at Oliver's feet and he sagged in the new thug's grip.

Sweenie removed his gun from Oliver's head and waved it at Adam.

"And don't think of trying anything. I'm leaving some of my men here until we're clear." The criminal grabbed Adam with a fist to his shirt and shoved him toward the door.

Adam and Sweenie disappeared and the room dropped into silence save for Oliver's ragged breathing.

Dalton's chest squeezed and his hands fisted when Adam left his sight. No fucking way was Sweenie a contest against Sphinx. The only way Sweenie could control Adam was to put him in chains along with armed guards. Guards like the guy holding the gun on Oliver.

The thug didn't even fucking blink. He just gave them a

flat, dead stare. Not only did the senator have crooks in the FBI, it appeared he had gone and hired professionals. The man staring back at him was a killer, through and through. He had no more care for Oliver's life than he did for a bug. Dalton could see it, and when a commotion outside of the steel door had the guy's eyes flickering that way, Dalton took advantage of it.

Simultaneously, laughter and hooting came from the back office where Jacob was located. At the noise, Oliver dropped to the floor, causing the killer's grip to adjust, and that was all Dalton needed.

He lunged in and snap-kicked the thug in the throat. Putting the full force of his weight into his other fist, Dalton punched the man in the heart.

The fucker crumbled.

Gunfire echoed from the outer room just before a familiar figure entered.

"You called for help?" Ex-Special Forces, Joshua Greene, stepped through the open door.

Relief washed over Dalton at the sight of their former commander. It made sense that Dave would call Greene since he lived the closest.

Before he could answer Greene, Ace sprang past him, racing for the back room.

"Take care of Oliver!" Dalton said, and while everything inside of him wanted to race after Adam, he charged after Ace.

The fact of the matter was, Jacob was more vulnerable than Adam right now.

Two men, twice Jacob's size, were beating and kicking the younger man. Jacob lay curled in a fetal position on the floor, protecting his head and stomach. Two other thugs stood laughing.

Ace went a bit mad.

Like a wrathful avenger bent on killing anything and anyone who stood in his way, Ace let out a howl upon entering the room.

Dalton kept up as best he could, but his boss had killed one of the laughing men before he could blink. Dalton dropped low and punched the second laughing guy in the junk, sending the man doubled over and puking on the floor. His hand cracked down on the guy's neck and he dropped like a stone into his own puke.

The two men who stood over Jacob didn't have time to even respond before Ace was on them. Ace picked up one and tossed him like a toy across the room. The guy had to be two hundred pounds or more and indented the wall when he hit before sliding down, out cold.

Dalton dodged in, attempting to help with the last man standing, but Ace closed his hand around the guy's neck and crushed his throat. It was a move not many men could achieve, but Ace was beyond reason.

Everything happened so fucking fast, the perps hadn't even had a chance to open fire.

Ace reached down and lifted Jacob to his feet. Murder filled their commander's eyes as he looked over Jacob's swollen lip and eye.

Without a word, Ace wiped the blood dripping from the corner of Jacob's mouth with his thumb. Dropping his hand, Ace gazed at Dalton over Jacob's dark-haired head.

"Go check on Oliver. I'll be right behind you."

Taking a few precious moments, Dalton zip-tied the hands and feet of the three perps who were still alive.

"You got it." He left his boss and the techie and re-entered the main room.

Greene and Oliver were nowhere in sight.

Dalton ran. Snagging his weapon from the small steps, he stepped through the broken wooden door and into the brewery's main room.

The scene had his heart jumping into his throat.

A few wounded customers lay scattered in the wreckage. Soot covered half of the room, more toward the bar. The smell of sulfur and gunpowder was heavy.

What the fuck had Greene done? Walked through a hail of bullets to get from the front door to the back room? It would be just like the guy to do just that. Dalton finally caught sight of Greene half carrying Oliver out the front entrance while Eagle and Link laid down cover fire.

Sirens filled the air and from the sound of it, it was both fire and rescue and the police.

An explosive device had gone off near the bar toward the front door, leaving that section of the brewery in shambles. A bullet slammed into the wood near his head and he dropped low.

Having confirmed where the rest of Pegasus was at the moment, he felt marginally relieved they appeared unharmed. The only one Dalton couldn't get a bead on was Hunter. Where the hell was their newest recruit?

Spotting the boots of Cooper, Dalton worked his way through the rubble toward the bartender. The man lay flat on his back on the floor with part of a wooden table covering him.

Most of the customers had fled in panic upon the thugs' entrance. Hopefully, Cooper's parents had made it out. Running in a hunch, he reached Cooper's body and cupped his hand beneath the man's armpits and pulled. Cooper slid from beneath the table and Dalton pulled until the bartender's body was around and behind the protection of the bar. Dead or not, Cooper didn't deserve to lay out in the open.

A groan from Cooper sent Dalton's heart slamming into his ribcage and he clamped his hand on Cooper's shoulder as the wave of relief swept over him.

"Hang tight, bud, help is coming."

Dalton lifted up and took aim and fired a round that plunged into a perp's calf. The man howled, wobbled, and dropped. Mason leaped, cat-like, and took out the guy.

A perp leaped at Mason and Gage growled, the sound traveling across the room. Gage lunged up and caught the man's hair before sending the guy's head into the wall with a brutal slam. Mason laughed, shook back his hair, and gave Gage a wide grin.

Tat, tat, tat.

Bullets peppered the area around Gage and Mason and the pair dove for cover again. Fucking hell, those two were going to give him gray hairs.

"Psst!" Eagle got his attention from across the space between the stage and the bar. "Someone took Adam out the front."

More bullets slammed into the area around Mason and Gage, and Dalton hesitated.

"Go," Link growled and sent several rounds into the wood where the perps had taken cover. His men had the remaining suspects pinned down.

Dalton wanted to stay and help, but he needed to get to Adam. From his vantage point, he had a clear shot to the front door.

Under cover of Link's gunfire, Dalton reached down, grabbed Cooper beneath his armpits, and pulled.

From the back, Ace came out of the wooden door and ran stooped over toward him. Without a word, his commander grabbed Cooper's feet.

"He's alive."

Relief swam in Ace's glittering gaze. Together, staying low, they carried Cooper across the short distance and through the open front door. Dalton kept going until they were around the wall and out of sight, next to the building.

EMTs ran in a crouch over to them.

"There was an explosion," Dalton told them and followed Ace toward the waiting police SUV. There, one of the officers broke away and approached.

"Sergeant Rail," Ace said.

"Ace, what the hell is going on?"

"Eagle, Link, Mason, and Gage are inside. There are two, maybe three, suspects that have them pinned down. If you go in behind shields, you should be able to take the perps out," Ace told Rail.

"I'm going to have to arrest everyone in there," Rail said, squinting at Ace.

"Then fucking take them into custody," Ace snarled, snapping a fresh clip into his nine-millimeter. "Just get in there and help."

"I need to go, one got away with someone," Dalton growled.

"Go," Ace ordered.

"I'll get your statement when you get back," Sergeant Rail told him before turning toward his team of trained SWAT officers.

While Pegasus was considered a top-secret unit, they worked closely with local PD to keep their actions somewhat on the up and up. Sometimes, it didn't always work that way, but they tried. Sometimes, people needed to die, and now was one of those times. He didn't need or want the local PD's help to find Adam because Dalton fully intended to kill Sweenie when he got his hands on him.

Now, he needed to find out where the hell they'd gone.

Sweenie had a ten, almost fifteen-minute head start, but if he knew Adam, he wasn't going to make it easy on Sweenie to get out of the area.

Dalton figured he had one ace in the hole.

Hunter was out there somewhere.

Making a left down the side of the building and into the wet alleyway, the shadows swallowed him.

CHAPTER THIRTY-ONE

Adam

"Y̲OU KNOW THEY'RE GOING TO ARREST OR KILL YOU, DON'T you?"

"Shut up." Sweenie shoved him again as they made their way down the dark alley.

Adam tested the handcuffs Sweenie had snapped around his wrists before yanking him into the brewery's main room. The scene had been pure carnage and Sweenie had used him as a human shield so Dalton's men couldn't get a shot.

"Just shoot!" Adam had shouted. "I won't press charges."

"Shut the fuck up!" Sweenie pressed the handgun barrel beneath his chin as they backed toward the front door.

Sweenie's men fired at Dalton's to give the guy cover.

Nobody from Pegasus fired until they left the building and then gunfire roared.

Sweenie made an annoyed sound in his throat when they turned another corner and again found it empty.

It had been the third corner they'd turned, the third alley that had come up empty.

"Whatcha looking for?" Adam smirked. "I doubt your transportation is still alive."

"I said shut the fuck up or I'll kill you here and bring him your body."

"Bring who my body? Black?"

The man said nothing.

"The senator?" Adam sneered.

Sweenie gave a start of surprise.

"Yeah, I know all about him and what he did. And so does the Secretary of Defense," Adam added.

"Just keep walking," the man snapped.

Adam moved forward and they turned a corner into another alley.

"I'll take it from here," Black said from the shadows.

"What? No, I want to see the senator. I want my money. I'll need it to dodge Pegasus," Sweenie snarled.

"All the money in the world won't save you from them," Adam murmured to Sweenie, but his gaze was locked with his former handler.

Black stepped into the light. A handgun glinted in his hands, and the guy wore all dark clothing.

"Sweenie?" Black said.

"Yes?"

It was the last word Sweenie spoke.

Snick, snick.

Black put two in Sweenie's heart and he crumpled to the ground. Adam lifted his eyes from the dark lump and stared at Black. He expected to be next, but Black waved the gun at him.

"Get moving."

"Oh, that's right. The senator wants to see me." Adam didn't budge.

"That's right," Black growled. "Now get moving."

"I don't have what he wants." He was of half a mind to tell Black what he'd told Sweenie—Pegasus knew everything. Instead, he held the last card close to his chest. It might just be the only thing keeping him alive. And he needed to stay alive to get out of this mess. Well, that and to see Dalton again.

He wasn't sure if Dalton could ever forgive him for lying by omission, but Adam thought he'd like to give earning the man's trust a try. Making up with Dalton would be the highlight of his life.

"Move," Black hissed. Growing impatient, the man stepped forward and shoved him.

Adam got moving toward the end of the alley and the street beyond.

A dark town car sat idling, the smoke from the exhaust pipe billowing in the damp night air. A yellowed streetlight cast an eerie glow through the smoke, giving the car a sinister look. If he got in that car, he'd be a dead man, but at least he'd get a face-to-face with the man who'd caused all this shit.

"So, it was you who blacklisted me," Adam murmured to Black. "You were the robotic voice on the phone who gave me the job?"

"I was," Black said with amusement in his voice. "You know, none of this would have happened if you would have just fucking handed over the flash drive and not looked at the contents."

"Well, call me fucking stupid then. I never do anything blindly. That was your first mistake, thinking I would follow along like a sheep."

LETHAL

The door to the town car opened, the wide, black hole gaping with only a small overhead light glowing inside.

"Yeah, I won't make that mistake again," Black snarled. "Now get in."

He slid into the car and fell into the cushiony seat; his senses were immediately assaulted with the smell of leather and expensive cologne.

Across from him sat a massive bodyguard type with a handgun resting on his thigh, the barrel pointed right at him. Next to the bodyguard sat the senator, with his blond hair, blue eyes, and a charming smile gracing his lips. Adam might have been fooled if it hadn't been for the cruel look in the man's eyes and the hands fisted on the top of his legs.

"Adam Campbell," the senator said.

Before he could tell the man to go fuck himself, Black's head was slammed into the metal of the car and yanked away. Something hard hit Adam's foot and he casually placed his foot over the small black object.

"Go!" the Senator shouted, and the car slammed forward with a squeal of the tires.

Adam got a quick look out the door at muscled shoulders and an attractive masculine face before the door was slammed shut. In that second before the door closed, the guy winked at him.

The man was the same one from Dalton's team that he'd run into in Arizona. He'd recognize that cut over the guy's eye anywhere. Adam could have laughed, but he whipped around instead and watched the sexy bastard plant a booted foot down on Black's face, pressing his former handler's cheek into the dirty concrete.

Turning around, Adam leaned back against the leather and gave the senator a smug look. He shifted a bit as if getting comfortable, but it was the hard object beneath his foot that he edged beneath the seat and out of sight.

"The cat's out of the bag. You're caught. You're going to jail," Adam said.

"You have no idea of who I am nor what I'm capable of." The senator's lip curled and the interior light flipped on inside.

"Black is caught. He'll be arrested for murder and I'm betting he'll sing like a canary about you." Adam smirked at the scumbag.

"He can sing all he wants. I'll have him eliminated in jail."

Adam squinted at the senator. Just how far did the man's corruption reach?

"Do you really think you're going to get away with this? You killed innocent people and you think you're gonna just walk away?"

The senator brushed at an imaginary piece of lint on his black jacket. "Politicians have been doing it since the beginning of time."

"Why didn't you just confess that you cheated to your wife?" It was the one thing he couldn't understand. People forgave others all the time for indiscretions.

The senator sneered. "I don't care about my wife. It's my reputation that's at stake. How would that look when I run for president someday?"

"God forbid."

Adam had to glance away. A glint in the senator's eyes looked a touch mad, and Adam knew better than to argue with a deranged person.

Gazing down at his handcuffed wrists, he wondered how long it would take Dalton to find him.

Because he was pretty sure the attractive guy had thrown a tracker at his feet.

CHAPTER THIRTY-TWO

Dalton

He came up on Hunter fast and found the guy heading back toward the office on foot with an older man.

"Who's this?" Dalton asked.

"This is the guy who set your Adam up." Hunter nudged the older man to keep walking.

"The handler," Dalton said, his tone flat. He chambered a bullet and walked right up to the man and put the end of the barrel to the handler's forehead. "You have two seconds to tell me where Adam is."

Black's eyes went wide with panic. "I don't know! I swear."

"He doesn't know," Hunter said, "but I have a way to find him."

Dalton had to be satisfied with that. For now. But before

he removed the gun from the man's head, he whispered, "He better be alive or you won't live."

Black swallowed hard, his whole body shaking.

● ● ◆

"A pager? You threw a god damned pager into the car?" Dalton gazed blankly at Hunter.

"Yep," Hunter drawled and stood leaning a hip on Jacob's desk.

Jacob's fingers clicked loudly in the room. Typing quicksilver fast, the techie was hacking into the pager company's database to track Adam's whereabouts.

"That's some quick thinking," Dalton muttered. He had to admit, as cocky as Hunter was, he was damned good.

Hunter's smile grew.

Gage scowled at Hunter. "Who the fuck carries a pager nowadays?"

Hunter snorted. "I use it when I don't want to be reached." Hunter pointed to Jacob's laptop. "And aren't you glad I do carry one?"

Gage snorted. "I guess you do all right for a pretty face."

"It's prettier than your mug," Hunter tossed back.

"Everyone is prettier than me," Gage responded.

"Fuck you," Mason said, sliding from where he sat on the top of a neighboring desk. "You both don't hold a candle to Dalton. He's the real pretty boy."

"Pipe down." Dalton scowled at Mason.

"Always mouthing off," Gage said and stifled a chuckle. The man earned a death glare from Mason. He'd recently gone back to his original hair color of blond. It did match the guy's blue eyes better.

Joshua Greene poked his head into the communications office. "Well, I'm out of here."

"Okay, bro." Mason gave Greene a fist bump.

"Thank you so much for your help," Dalton said and shook Greene's hand in a tight grip.

"Anytime. I'm just down the street." Greene tossed a glance at Mason. "Will we see you Sunday?"

"Sure, can I bring someone?" Mason's smile grew.

Gage shoved from his shoulder lean against the door and walked out. A short silence rang through the room. Dalton squinted at Mason and shook his head. Mason glared at him before turning back to Greene.

"Of course, you can bring someone." Greene pulled his brother-in-law into a hard hug and ruffled the man's blond hair.

That Greene wasn't on the ground for encroaching on Mason's personal space was a testament to how close the pair were. It made sense, though, since Greene was married to Mason's twin brother.

"I got it!" Jacob shoved back and pointed to the monitor.

The city map came up and a small red dot pulsed on the screen. Dalton shoved a fresh clip into his nine-millimeter.

"It's a good damned thing your pager comes with a tracking device. That's where it is," Jacob told Hunter with a cheeky grin.

"That pager is state-of-the-art." Hunter snorted and lifted a finger beneath Jacob's chin. "Got some fierce bruising going on there."

Dalton shoved into a jacket. "Who's going with?"

Jacob jerked his head away from Hunter's touch and scowled at the guy. "I'm not a baby."

Hunter laughed. "I didn't say you were."

"Get the fuck on the road." Ace's growling words filled with ice came from the doorway.

Hunter straightened up from Jacob's desk like a fire had just lit his ass.

Dalton moved past Ace and out into the bullpen. At his appearance, Eagle and Link both shoved up from their desks, grabbing jackets and guns, and flanked him.

Before Dalton, along with Eagle and Link, reached the steel door, Hunter, Gage, Mason, and Jacob were all heading their way.

He stared at Jacob, and the young man tipped his chin up and squinted as if silently daring him to say a word.

"I have the laptop." Jacob held up the small computer.

The red dot glowed on the screen.

"You have no weapons training."

"Fuck you, Dalton," Jacob snapped right back. "You know my three dads are part of Phoenix. I've had training. I owe these guys some payback."

Dalton clenched his teeth and gazed over Jacob's head to Ace.

From the look on his boss's face, Ace had already tried to forbid Jacob from coming.

It hadn't worked and the stubborn look on Jacob's face told Dalton the young man wasn't budging on this. Dalton needed that damned laptop to find Adam.

"You stay in the fucking car," Dalton growled at Jacob, out of patience and out of time. Adam needed him and he had no more time for any bullshit.

Jacob handed the computer to Hunter while he shrugged into a leather bomber jacket that was hanging on a peg by the door. The jacket was Ace's and swallowed Jacob, making him look even more vulnerable than the bruises on his young face.

LETHAL

Reaching the brewery's main room, Dalton found a couple of detectives along with Sergeant Rail going over the shambles of the brewery bar area. Cooper was already at the hospital along with his parents—it was minute by minute if Cooper would live or not.

"Well, hello there, handsome," Hunter said when they converged farther into the main room and started picking their way through the debris.

Sergeant Rail gazed at Hunter. Rail looked like he'd swallowed a golf ball, and it wasn't the first time he'd seen that look on the sergeant's face. Rail had been about to arrest them all when Dalton and Hunter had shown up back at the scene with CIA Agent Black in cuffs.

"This is the real culprit," Hunter told Rail, shoving Black forward. "I want you to call your captain before you arrest any of the men left in this room." The only people remaining were the men of Pegasus.

"Why would I call my captain?" Rail snapped.

"Because he's my big brother," Hunter said with a casual, flirty smile.

Rail blinked, swallowed hard, and blinked again before scowling. Punching in a number, Rail lifted the cell phone to his ear and told his captain the situation.

"Yes, sir. Of course, sir. He's right here." Looking white as a sheet, Rail held the cell phone out to Hunter.

Hunter took the phone. "Bro?" Shouting came from the receiver so loud that Hunter pulled the phone away from his face.

"Love you too, Bro. Gotta go." Ending the call, Hunter had handed the phone back to Rail.

"You seven look like trouble," Rail returned flatly, giving them all a bitter look. "Don't be shooting up my city again."

"We wouldn't dream of it," Mason said with a snicker.

Dalton kept on walking until he was out the door and

behind the wheel of the team's black SUV. It fit the unit comfortably and without Ace in the passenger seat, Eagle took over that spot.

Dalton punched the gas and burned rubber away from the Pegasus building. The tires slipped on the wet pavement before catching purchase. Fear soured his throat. The senator could have already killed Adam and dumped his body.

"Take a left on 2nd Street," Jacob said from the back seat, jerking his thoughts away from the rabbit hole.

Dalton squeezed the steering wheel.

Hang on, Adam. I'm coming.

CHAPTER THIRTY-THREE

Adam

It was the longest hour of his life.

Thank fuck they hadn't ditched the car with the tracker Dalton's man had put inside. The vehicle sat off to the side near the loading dock inside of a large, cold warehouse.

Adam tested the bonds that kept his hands behind his back. The bodyguard had shoved him into a hardbacked wooden chair and zip-tied each ankle to the chair's legs. The handcuffs were removed next.

At that point, Adam made a move. He cracked his forehead into the bodyguard's head with a hard slam. The guy stumbled back with a grunt, but the size of the behemoth kept him from going down. All Adam had managed to do was topple sideways in the chair.

The giant lifted him, chair and all, upright and Adam braced when the backhand hit him hard and blood filled his mouth. Pain lanced through his face and he spat blood at the guy.

The bodyguard stepped away, but it splattered his boots. Moving in again, the man roughly yanked his arms behind his back and zip-tied them to the wooden chair. The guy then stepped around in front of him, and Adam braced himself for another blow. Instead, the guy fisted his hair and yanked his head back, neck straining. The bodyguard looked down in his face with cold eyes.

"Be good, pretty boy. I would hate to break this jaw and the senator not get his answers."

"We wouldn't want that," he rasped, holding back the shiver of revulsion when the behemoth cupped a hand at his throat and nudged a large, thick thigh between his legs.

"Knock it off, Lars," the senator said. The man's voice had come from somewhere to his right.

Lars released the grip on his hair and Adam straightened his neck gently before flicking his eyes around, taking in his surroundings, trying to get an idea of where he was and what he could use to get out of this situation. He noted five other thugs, all armed, but suspected there were probably more.

The chair beneath him was wood, but it was thick and sturdy. Although, he had a feeling he could break it if push came to shove.

"All right, Mr. Campbell." The senator came around into his line of sight, dragging a matching wooden chair. He placed the chair several feet from him and took a seat. "Who did you give the flash drive to?"

"I have it hidden. If anything happens to me, it goes to the media."

Oh, the man didn't like that, and Adam could have laughed. It was all about this bastard's reputation, after all.

"Where is it hidden?"

"If I told you that, then you'd just kill me." Adam shrugged.

The senator licked his lips and rubbed at his hands with a small white cloth. "You're going to die either way. Why not go out quick and painless?"

"Senator?" he said.

"Yes?" The man's face lit up.

"Go fuck yourself."

The man's face darkened into an ugly scowl and he gave the bodyguard a nod.

Adam braced himself, tightened his gut, and turned his face away.

Snick, snick.

The guy's punch never landed. Instead, his body crumpled to the ground.

Yes! The cavalry had arrived.

The senator scrambled from his chair and ran with two of his men to take cover.

Adam threw his body to the side and the chair, along with him, went crashing painfully to the ground again, but at least he was out of the line of fire. Automatic gunfire echoed in the large warehouse as the senator's men opened fire.

Hard hands gripped the back of his toppled chair and he was slid across the concrete floor and pulled behind a stack of wooden pallets. Something hard swiped at the thick zipties at his hands and then his arms were free.

Dalton came around in a crouch and sliced free his legs.

Adam rolled until he was away from the chair and came up into a hunch, keeping low and out of sight.

"Did they hurt you?"

"Nah." He gave Dalton a grin and then checked the clip on the handgun Dalton handed him. "But I did want to pay back the big one that went down." He nodded to the dead bodyguard.

"Sorry?" Dalton smirked.

"You don't look sorry." He snickered and leaned in to kiss the man on the lips.

"I'm not," Dalton grunted and pressed into the kiss hard before pulling back. "Let's get that bastard."

"He ran this way," Adam said and ran stooped over down the long aisle of pallets. Reaching the end, he waited there with Dalton. Across in the other aisle crouched a blond guy with another hulking man behind him. The hulking man had a fist to the back of the blond guy's shirt as if holding him back from something. A quick glance ahead told Adam it was a group of four armed men sheltered behind a metal bench cabinet returning fire.

Dalton leaned up to his ear. "We will lay down cover fire," Dalton growled, holding his gaze.

Adam gave a nod and on Dalton's count, they both fired at the metal bench. The blond man and the hulk darted from their cover and ran, getting closer to the metal bench. Two other men slipped through the dimly lit warehouse and Adam lifted his gun.

Dalton put a hand on his arm. "They're mine."

"Just checking," he whispered back and again fired at the metal cabinet. This part of the warehouse was a dead end with no sign of the senator.

"You got this?" Adam asked impatiently. "I want the senator."

With those words, he melted away from Dalton and headed in the other direction. The senator must be making his way to the loading dock. In seconds, Dalton was at his side, making him smile.

"What's the plan?"

"My guess is he's headed back to the car. It's his escape route," Adam said.

When his words ended, an engine revved and tires squealed.

"Shit!" he hissed and lunged toward the sound with Dalton on his six. He ran across the warehouse and reached the loading dock when the senator's town car barreled past, heading for the closed metal door.

Adam pulled the trigger. The gun jumped in his hand with each round that plunged into the windows of the car.

"Bulletproof!" he snarled.

Dalton dropped to one knee and took aim. First one tire blew out and then the other. Dalton was fucking lethal with his aim. The car jerked one way and then the other before it fishtailed and spun in a full circle. It crashed sideways into the door of the warehouse. Two men poured out from the vehicle and opened fire. He and Dalton lunged for cover behind a stack of paper supplies.

Fuck, they were pinned!

Dalton's other men were busy battling it out on the other side of the warehouse, the echo of that gun battle ringing in the distance. The senator scrambled from the town car under the protection of the two guards.

Bang! Bang!

Both of the senator's guards toppled to the ground, one with a chest shot and the other in the head. Dalton seemed to have a plethora of operatives at his disposal.

"Get on the fucking ground or you're next," Jacob yelled, his dark, curly hair askew. The gun he held pointed at the senator.

"Jesus Christ!" Dalton muttered, staring in amazement at Jacob. "Fuck."

The senator didn't argue, he dropped to his knees and laced his hands behind his head.

Adam shoved out from his spot and approached where the senator was kneeling.

"Nice shooting," Adam told Jacob.

"Thanks." Dimples flashed along with a quick, shy smile before Jacob handed a bemused Dalton the gun.

"Who gave you the gun?" Dalton asked gruffly.

"Eagle."

"Thank fuck it wasn't Hunter," Dalton said.

"Why?" The young hottie frowned.

"Because Ace would have killed him."

"And he won't kill Eagle?" Jacob asked.

"Maybe," Dalton returned gruffly and zip-tied the senator's hands behind his back and pressed the mic in his ear.

"Report."

"All clear." The voice came from the area where the metal bench had been, and Dalton's men appeared, along with two perps.

"Two dead," a large man said, shoving forward the two perps in handcuffs.

"And it looks like two more are down," one of the men said with a smirking grin at Jacob.

"Good thing you gave me the gun. I saved these two." Jacob waved at him and Dalton.

Dalton scowled and his jaw ticked. Adam felt a snicker rising to the surface.

All of Dalton's men, the men of Pegasus, stepped out of the shadows and into the dim lighting of the warehouse. Holy fuck. Where did they grow these guys? Were all the men of Pegasus sexy as hell?

"That's Hunter." Dalton pointed to the man who had placed the tracker at his feet.

"We've met before." Adam smirked at the operative who had almost caught him in Arizona.

Hunter grinned and lightly touched the cut above his eye. "That we have."

"Thank you," Adam said, holding Hunter's gaze.

"No problem." Hunter ducked his head and walked over to punch the button that would open the big rolling doors of the warehouse.

"That's Eagle," Dalton said, bringing Adam's attention back to the group. "And he might be looking at his last days on earth for arming Jacob with a gun," Dalton finished with a hard look at Eagle.

Adam gave Eagle a smile.

"The big guy behind Eagle is Link. The blond is Mason and you know Gage," Dalton said, pointing to the rough-looking, musclebound man standing off to the side. Blood dripped down the side of Gage's t-shirt. The blond man, the one called Mason, appeared to have just noticed the blood and long strides took him to Gage's side.

Gage ignored Mason with a flat look and stalked over to pull the senator to his feet, marching him out the open warehouse door without a word.

"Well, he's lovely," Mason said with a sigh.

"This… is Adam," Dalton said to the rest of the unit. The proud tone in Dalton's voice had him beaming a smile.

"Your Adam?" Eagle said to Dalton in a teasing tone of voice.

"Yep, mine." Dalton slipped an arm around his shoulders and pulled him close.

"So, the Sphinx has been well and truly caught," Mason said with a snicker and offered his hand after dragging his eyes from Gage's disappearing form.

Gazing up at Dalton for a moment, Adam laughed and shook Mason's hand. "Yeah, and I don't mind a damned bit."

"Ah! Here it is."

Hunter's voice drew Adam's gaze and the man emerged from the town car holding up... Was that a pager?

"Who in the world carries a pager?" Adam asked.

They all laughed at his bewildered tone.

"Don't be hating on the pager," Hunter said with a smug look, tucking it away.

"I wouldn't dream of it," Adam said, joining in with the laughter.

CHAPTER THIRTY-FOUR

Dalton

H E SAT AT THE TABLE IN THE BRIGHT KITCHEN OF HIS SMALL apartment. Sunlight glinted through the yellow curtains and sent flecks of onyx shining through Adam's hair.

Adam stood at the stove, cooking them rolled oats and wearing only tight blue briefs and a white t-shirt. Dalton could have sat in that brightly lit kitchen all day. Watching Adam could quickly become his favorite pastime.

"What did Ace say?" Adam asked again for the tenth time since the phone call twenty minutes ago.

"He said he wants us in the office in an hour," he patiently answered again.

Ace had ordered him to take the day off after they'd apprehended the senator, and Dalton had done just that. He'd coaxed Adam into coming to his apartment.

They would eventually need to go into the FBI office

and give statements, but Adam hadn't been arrested. That didn't mean Adam could leave the immediate area until the FBI wrapped up the case, but at least the FBI hadn't locked Adam up. Dalton suspected the SecDef had something to do with that.

His phone buzzed and he glanced at it, giving a sigh of relief.

"Who's that?"

"It's Hunter. Cooper lost his hearing in one ear, but he's going to pull through."

"I'm so glad."

"Me too. Any word on Oliver?"

"No, not yet." Dalton rubbed a hand down his face.

"I wonder what Ace wants us for?" Adam stirred the oats, teeth cleaving into the side of his bottom lip.

Dalton shoved away from the table and went to Adam. "It means Ace wants us in the office. Don't think too much into it." He wrapped Adam up tightly.

"Let's go back to bed instead," Adam said with a groan and gyrated his ass back against him.

"As tempting as that is, we shouldn't be late," he groaned and nuzzled the side of Adam's neck.

They'd spent the past twenty-four hours talking and making love on every surface of his apartment, and he'd finally gotten Adam to commit to him.

Sort of.

Their relationship was contingent upon the outcome of the FBI's findings. He hated it, but he knew Adam wouldn't start another relationship with him if the guy thought he was going to jail. Adam had come up with some bullshit thing about leaving Dalton free to find love. Which was utterly ludicrous. He'd never find another love like Adam, and he had told the man so.

"What if it's bad?"

"Whatever happens, we'll face it together," he murmured into the side of Adam's neck.

"Mmm, my big bad wolf. Have I told you I love you today?" Adam said breathlessly and turned in his arms.

Dalton's heart lurched and then slammed against his ribs. "No, but I know, cupcake."

Adam fisted his fingers in his hair and drew his mouth down. The kiss was hot and heated and his head grew foggy.

Breakfast was forgotten.

Running his hands down Adam's back, he cupped his ass and lifted. Adam wrapped his legs around his waist. Dalton flipped off the burner beneath the pot of oats and strode back toward the bedroom.

Fuck the meeting.

He had much better things to do with his time.

"You better fucking hurry," Adam hissed, his voice full of need, making Dalton smile as he nuzzled Adam's neck.

Long strides took him down the hallway and into his bedroom and once there, he tossed Adam down onto the bed. The man stretched, arms flung high over his head, the t-shirt riding up and showing the hard bulge straining the skimpy blue briefs.

Dalton's smile grew and Adam's own lips curved. "Are you waiting for an invitation?" Adam teased.

"Maybe," Dalton said huskily and leaned over, brushing a kiss to Adam's lips.

Dalton wanted to take it slow, but the heat that exploded between them whenever they touched raced up and he was a goner. He fought to get Adam out of his t-shirt. Adam rose up and started yanking at Dalton's shirt and pants.

At one point, Dalton fell on his ass and a laughing Adam tugged the legs of his sweats to pull them off. Dalton tossed

Adam's t-shirt to the floor and then snatched more condoms and lube from the nightstand.

Adam's sexy laugh filled the room. He reached for Adam and sleek, muscled skin met his.

Dalton stretched out over the man and took his mouth in another slow kiss, tasting Adam's lips over and over. He slid his thigh between Adam's legs and pressed into the man's balls before he reached down and gripped Adam's hard, thrusting cock. His tongue tangled with Adam's tongue while he slowly stroked the wet, engorged head of the man's cock with his thumb.

"Nnnnh fuck," Adam groaned into his mouth.

Dalton released Adam's cock and snatched up the lube. Rising up, he dumped some into his hand and traced his fingers down past Adam's balls and along the crease of his ass. Reaching Adam's entrance, he massaged it until Adam was writhing on the bed, fisting the sheets.

"You sure you're not too sore?"

"It's my turn," Adam hissed and a fierce light filled his eyes.

That was true. They'd taken turns through the night and his ass was as sore as he imagined Adam's was.

"Plus, I will throttle you if you don't hurry up," Adam growled.

He chuckled and pressed into Adam's hole, easing his cock inside. Adam sighed, closed his eyes, and wrapped his long legs around him.

When Adam urged him faster, Dalton didn't argue nor did he wait. His man was just as hungry as he was.

All the other shit could wait.

This right here was worth shutting the world out.

CHAPTER THIRTY-FIVE

Adam

He gripped Dalton by the shoulders when the man's cock pistoned deep, and wrapped his legs tightly around Dalton's hips, forcing him deeper.

Dalton groaned.

Adam gave an answering groan when Dalton's hard length slid as far as possible into his ass.

"Oh, fuck yeah," Adam gasped harshly, adjusting to the cock's length before placing his open mouth on the sweat slicked skin of Dalton's neck.

"Fuck," Dalton muttered when he tongued the man's salty jugular.

Adam smiled and sucked up a mark. Sue him. The thought of Dalton wearing his mark sent his cock into overload and he gyrated, grinding his dick up into Dalton's stomach.

Dalton growled and slammed in, and Adam let his eyes fall closed when the thick, hot cock drove deep. Dalton lifted upward and pulled Adam's legs from around his waist, pushing his thighs wide and his knees outward. From that point, Dalton looked down at his cock thrusting in and out of him.

Oh fuck. Adam gripped the bedsheets, tossing his head back and forth with each thrust.

When Dalton paused and pulled out, a growl welled up in Adam's throat and his eyes flew open to catch and hold Dalton's.

The man grinned, meeting his eyes, and scooted back. Gentle hands brought his legs together and then Adam was flipped onto his stomach.

"Oh yeah, fuck yeah," he moaned, pressing his face into the pillow when his legs and ass were spread wide. Dalton crowded up behind him and slipped his thick cock back inside.

When Dalton slipped deep and knocked against his prostate, Adam knew he wouldn't last long in this position.

Dalton gripped him at the waist and pulled him to his knees. A hand pressed his back down and his chest went to the bed, leaving his ass high. Adam fisted the sheets by his head and hung on.

Sliding deep, Dalton's long cock filled every inch of his ass. Sliding his cock out slowly, Dalton pushed back in and repeated the move until Adam screamed a low, guttural sound, only muffled by the pillow. At his noise, Dalton sank in and stayed there, grinding his hips and cock into his ass.

So fucking deep.

When Dalton started a brutal pace, Adam howled. Over and fucking over, Dalton fucked him thoroughly and then reached a hand beneath his stomach and gripped his cock. Adam grunted and thrust into Dalton's tight fist, fucking the man's hand quickly.

When Dalton squeezed his cock, Adam exploded. He spiraled and shuddered. His body convulsed and his cock jerked in Dalton's fist before spilling come onto the sheets beneath him.

Releasing his grip, Dalton grabbed Adam's hips and started a hard pounding in his ass. Adam hung on as his own orgasm shuddered through him.

With one last slam home, Dalton curled forward over his back. Panting, the man roamed his lips along his shoulder and neck. The next moment, Dalton groaned, spasmed, and jerked before filling the condom.

They were getting tested next week! Fuck the latex-covered bullshit, he wanted to feel Dalton and vice versa.

Dalton's rapid breath swept near his ear before the man eased sideways and flopped to his back onto the bed, chest heaving. Adam turned onto his side and sprawled next to Dalton.

The room filled with the sound of their slowed breathing, combined with the occasional vehicle passing on the street outside.

"Want to talk?" Dalton curled an arm around him and pulled him closer.

"About what?"

"Anything. The fact that your handler blacklisted you?"

"Black. God, I never thought for a second that he'd turn on me. I mean, I've been to the man's house. I've eaten dinner with his family. He has two kids for fuck's sake. What an idiot."

"I'm sorry, babe." Dalton kissed his head.

"It hurts," he admitted. "He also tried to make me take the fall for Agent Farnsworth's death in Alaska."

"I know."

They laid like that for a long moment before Adam rolled and lifted onto an elbow to gaze into Dalton's eyes.

"How is Gage?"

"The bullet was a through and through. He needed stitches, but it's not life-altering like Cooper."

"I'm sorry about Cooper."

"Yeah. With the loss of hearing in one ear, I'm not sure where that leaves him."

"Does he need to be actively in the field? Can't he stay behind the bar and guard the place? From the way you talk about him, the guy sounds like a badass," Adam pointed out.

"That's true. I just don't know if he'll want his wings clipped."

"Well, there's time. We should stop by the hospital on our way to or from the office," he said.

"About the office," Dalton started, paused, and then took a deep breath. "Come work for Pegasus."

He huffed a laugh and sat up, crisscrossing his legs on the bed. "Don't you need to ask Ace before you go inviting me to be part of the team?"

"Well, yeah, but if you're not okay with it, then I won't bother asking Ace," Dalton said reasonably.

"I don't know. I haven't thought past being a CIA agent. I mean, I thought about quitting once I was blacklisted, but now that Black and the senator are behind bars, I wouldn't need to quit when my name's cleared."

"No… you wouldn't, but you could."

Adam studied Dalton for a moment. "Last night, you spoke of commitment, and I agreed. What does that look like? Are you asking me to move in here? You talked about a white picket fence with animals and kids."

"I did and I do. Yes, I want to live together. We can get a house."

"Here in Southern California?" He wondered if Dalton realized that the CIA sent him all over the world.

"Well..." Dalton sighed and rolled to sit up. "I know this sounds selfish, but yeah...here in SoCal. I have obligations to Pegasus, but give me time and I'll work out a solution. Then we can live anywhere."

His heart squeezed in his chest. Dalton was willing to give up Pegasus for him?

"Dalton?"

"Yeah?"

"I love you so much."

Dalton cupped his cheek and brushed a thumb through the stubble along his jawline. "I love you too." The man's forehead creased.

"You won't need to leave your job. I can work from anywhere. Can you give me time to think over the offer of Pegasus?"

"Of course." A fierce light sparked in Dalton's whiskey-colored eyes.

They really were perfectly matched. Of course, they'd argue and have squabbles, but he knew in his heart that wouldn't stand in their way of happiness.

"And as far as getting a new place?"

"Yeah?"

"Let's go house hunting."

"You're on." Dalton's smile was so bright, it made his chest ache.

Tears stung Adam's eyes and he didn't think he could get any happier until Dalton's next words.

"Marry me."

CHAPTER THIRTY-SIX

Dalton

"**Y**ES."

Adam had said yes, and the word still rang in his ears and through his heart. The love of his life had said yes and they were getting married.

They were late to the Pegasus office, but only by a couple of hours.

In their defense, they'd stopped by the hospital on the way to Pegasus with flowers in hand for Cooper.

They were turned away when they asked about Oliver's condition. It was disheartening, but the head nurse was very firm on giving information to family only.

● ● ●

Stepping through the steel doors of Pegasus, the bullpen was filled with more than just his team.

A man—all, big, and mean looking—stood in the middle of the room taking up most of the space. Dalton didn't often need to physically look up to meet someone's gaze, but he did with this man, and frankly, it was intimidating.

Another stranger sat on a nearby desk, and if he wasn't mistaken, the man's hair hung halfway down his back. It was hard to tell from this angle, but he'd bet money on it. Both men oozed authority and danger, and his fingers itched to pull his gun from the waistband of his pants, but he held back on account of his boss.

Ace stood in the doorway of his office and Dalton held his boss's gaze from across the room. Dalton didn't approach the unfolding scene because something in Ace's gaze held him in place. He squeezed Adam's hand to keep him at his side. Adam must have sensed the turbulence in the room and went completely still next to him.

"Is that everything?"

Another man, this one wearing a suit that probably cost three times his mortgage, walked out of the communications room with Jacob.

"No, that's not everything," Jacob responded impatiently.

"It doesn't matter," the suit said with a hand beneath Jacob's elbow. "We will get the rest later."

The one with the long hair stood from his seat on the desk. At the same time, Eagle and Link both shoved from their shoulder leans against the wall.

"Look," Jacob snapped at the man in a suit and then spun on the massive mountain in the middle of the room before sending a glare at the long-haired one. "I appreciate your concerns, but this—" Jacob lifted a hand to the bruises on his own face and chin, "—is a hazard of the job."

Ah, a lightbulb went on. These men were Jacob's dads. Holy fuck. They worked for Phoenix. The original unit of all badasses. As a twin unit, men of Pegasus reported to the same chief, Giovanni Rossi, so Dalton had taken the time to memorize names and faces. Roscoe, the suit, was former FBI. The big one was known only as Storm, and the long-haired, gorgeous one they called Wild.

"No, that's not a hazard of the job," Storm snarled, his voice quiet, the graveled tone reverberating in the room. Dalton tensed and Ace gave a slight shake of his head. Wild put a hand on Storm's arm and the man calmed immediately. It was amazing to see the guy's demeanor change and gray eyes flash lovingly at Wild.

"We're only concerned about you," Roscoe quietly told Jacob.

"Then why don't you ask me what I want instead of coming in here and yanking me away from the only place I want to be, treating me as if I were a teenager instead of almost twenty-one?"

Roscoe appeared to be at a loss for words, as was Storm. Wild, on the other hand, stepped forward and pulled Jacob into a hug before turning the young man to face the other two parents.

"Jacob, tell us what you want," Wild said.

Jacob's bright blue eyes slid to Ace. For several moments, nobody spoke. Storm tensed and Roscoe made a sound in his throat.

"I want you three to quit treating me like a kid," Jacob snapped and pulled from Wild.

Marching over to stand in front of Ace, Jacob tipped his head back to gaze up into Ace's face. The tension between the two washed through the room. Storm's hands fisted and

Wild curled both hands around one of Storm's arms. Roscoe shoved his hands deep into his pockets.

"I'm taking a two-week vacation to think about things," Jacob said and waited for Ace to respond.

When Ace nodded, Jacob continued. "That gives you two weeks to get your head out of your ass and think about things too. I will be working in the field when I get back. If you can't accept that, then I'll have to go somewhere else," Jacob finished with a firm tone in his voice.

Dalton noticed pride flash in Wild and Roscoe's eyes. Storm, well, he looked like he wanted to kill Ace.

"Let's go." Roscoe stepped up to Jacob and drew the young man away from Ace. "I'll be calling you." Roscoe gave Ace a warning look before turning toward the door.

At that point, Dalton figured it was safe to move and eased him and Adam away from the steel door.

Silence rang through the room when Jacob and his dads left.

"Well," Mason quipped. "That was lovely."

"Fuck me." Eagle let out a breath. "I wouldn't want to meet those three fuckers in a dark alley."

"Same," Hunter agreed.

"So... is this normal?" Adam piped up from the spot at his side.

Dalton slid his arm around Adam's shoulders. "No. We don't normally have this many visitors."

Adam snickered and Dalton gave a rueful smile.

"All right, have a seat," Ace said over the laughter in the room.

Once everyone was situated, Ace leaned against a desk in front of them.

"Cooper will make a full recovery. With the loss of his hearing in one ear, he won't be returning to active duty per se. The doctors say it could be temporary hearing loss. Right now, it's a wait and see. Instead, he'll be taking over the running of the brewery as manager. Cooper, along with Peter and some new staff, will make sure no one but customers get through the front door again."

They didn't have a brewery manager; Ace usually filled in. It made sense to Dalton to hire someone, and he couldn't think of a better person than Cooper.

"The bullet that pierced Gage was a through and through," Ace continued.

"Where is Gage?" Dalton asked, not seeing the man in the room.

"He's currently at home. Gage asked for some leave time and I've granted that. When he gets back from the leave, I'm reassigning him to the field. So, I expect we won't see much of him here in the office."

Dalton slid a glance toward Mason. At the news, the man's face had gone pale, hands curled into fists on the top of his knees, but his eyes stayed locked on Ace.

"Dalton, I'll go over the specifics with you next week."

Dalton nodded at Ace.

"As for Oliver Rains. He made it through the night. His gunshot wound is substantial and he has a slight fracture in his leg. Although he is out of commission, he has agreed to join Pegasus. He wants to say a few words." Ace snapped up the remote and pushed the button, but the screen stayed dark. Ace punched several buttons and finally, the monitor flashed on. It took a few moments before Ace got the video call going of Oliver sitting up in a hospital bed.

"Hey guys." Oliver gave them a cheeky grin, his unshaven face pale, his hair askew, but he looked really good for a man who'd been shot. "Look for me to hobble in there in about two weeks. I wanted to take this opportunity to say…don't let Eagle eat all the snacks."

Eagle snorted and then laughed. "Always thinking about your stomach."

Dalton laughed along with the rest of the group. Eagle, Link, and Oliver went way back—the three men had served under the same colonel during their time in the Army Special Forces.

"Link?" Oliver called.

"Yeah?"

"I'm putting you in charge. Of snack details. I'll want lots of sweets and chocolate. Preferably together."

"I'll see what I can do," Link said good-naturedly.

"Oh, and Ace? I want a box of multi-colored markers." Oliver pointed to the pristine white of his leg cast. "Because yeah, I'll be wanting pictures colored of naked—" Oliver barely got that out before the phone was taken from him.

"Okay, getting loopy, are we? Time for a rest," a deep voice said from off-screen, and then an attractive face came into view.

"Guys, meet Lieutenant Maddox Stone," Eagle introduced and waited for the group to respond before asking. "How's Oliver really doing?"

"He's fine. General Rhine and Dillon are taking him home with them to recuperate," Maddox said.

"Good."

"Hey, we're having a poker night, you and Link down?"

"Wouldn't miss it," Eagle responded for both of them.

"I'll send you the details," Maddox said and ended the call.

The screen went dark and Ace fumbled with the remote and finally turned it off. Working the monitor had been Jacob's job.

"Adam?" Ace tossed the remote to the desk with a clatter.

"Yes?" Adam jerked up straight in his chair.

"You've been cleared of all charges. The SecDef should be calling you in person to tell you just that. Also, you can rejoin the CIA at your own pace."

Adam blinked at Ace and then tossed Dalton a glance. Dalton smiled.

"Thank you." Adam's response sounded so heartfelt, and Dalton rubbed at the ache in his chest.

"Of course, I'm hoping that you'll tell them to go fuck themselves and come work for me," Ace responded.

Chuckles filled the room and Dalton glanced around at the expectant faces gazing at Adam. He didn't want his man feeling pressured to join. Reaching over, he slid his fingers between Adam's own.

"You can take your time to answer. It doesn't need to be today," Dalton murmured.

"I don't need time," Adam said and turned to Ace. "I accept."

Ace released what sounded like a sigh of relief and cracked the first smile Dalton had seen from the man in a long time.

"I have to admit, Adam, I'll need your computer skills until Jacob returns."

"Not a problem," Adam responded. "Whatever you need."

Dalton let his smile widen. His man was a computer expert. Not up to Jacob's caliber, maybe, but not many people in the world could hold a candle to Jacob when it came to modern technology.

Ace rubbed at his chin. "I'm sure you've felt the tension between myself and Jacob. I'll be honest and tell you right now that I'm not comfortable with him in the field. I have my reasons. With that said, I'll need to take it one day at a time to figure out what I'm going to do when he gets back from his vacation, so bear with me."

He was sure the tension was from other things, but he sure as hell wasn't going to say anything.

"You got it, boss," Dalton drawled and swept his eyes around the room.

Every other person in the room nodded in agreement.

"Whatever you need," Mason said.

"Right now?" Ace caught Mason's eyes. "I don't want to see you back in this place until after the New Year."

Dalton turned to Adam and smiled. "And that's our cue," he said and made no attempt to keep his voice quiet.

Chuckles swept round the room.

"What's on the agenda?" Link asked them, grabbing his jacket.

"House hunting." Adam held up a stack of brochures he'd snagged from the gas station on the way in.

"Oh," Dalton called out, and the men in the room all paused. "I just want to let you know that I've proposed marriage to Adam, and he's accepted."

"Well, shit!" Eagle hooted and offered his fist up for a fist bump.

Link gave him a slap on the back and Adam a hug once Mason was done hugging Adam. Ace smiled and came forward to shake his hand.

"Congratulations," Ace said. "When's the day?"

"We haven't decided," Adam said with a laugh.

"Yeah, give us some time to enjoy the engagement part," Dalton grumbled.

"Oh, we need to have an engagement party," Eagle said.

"That's up to Dalton," Adam said with a smile, returning Eagle's hug.

"I'll call my mom," Dalton said, lifting Adam's hand to his lips. "My family will be thrilled."

"Another trip to Alaska?" Link said.

"No, we'll keep it local," Dalton responded. "My family will fly in."

"I'd like that," Adam said and squeezed his hand tightly.

Ace, who had disappeared into his office, reemerged with a bottle of unopened red wine. He popped the cork and produced several clear plastic cups.

Mason took the bottle from Ace once it was open and poured a round in the cups.

All glasses were lifted high and faces gazed in his direction.

Dalton turned to hold Adam's eyes.

"I've been waiting for you a long time. Ever since I screwed up as a kid. I promise I won't make that mistake again." He tapped his cup to Adam's cup.

"I'm holding you to that," Adam said with a laugh and did that silly thing where you link your arms around each other's before you drink.

It was cute as hell and Dalton didn't mind a fucking bit that they might appear corny.

If corny kept Adam in his life, then bring it on.

EPILOGUE

One month later
Dalton

"Yes, I know Mom." Dalton pulled his mother into a tight hug and gave his dad a *help me* look.

"That's enough, Leslie," Brian said with a soft stroke to his wife's bright hair.

Leslie sniffled, pulling from Dalton's arms. "I'm so darned happy. I thought this day would never come." She squeezed his cheeks.

"Wait until their wedding day," Mary joked. "She'll be inconsolable then."

"Oh shush!" Leslie sent her daughter a scolding look.

"Here, Mom, hold the baby." Renee stepped up and handed his mother the newborn.

"Oh, oh… come to grandma. Yes, you're such a good

baby," Leslie cooed and scooped the tiny bundle into her arms.

His niece had come two weeks earlier than planned, and Dalton could have kissed Renee at that moment; his sister was a lifesaver. She gave him a smile and wink.

"I think she's hungry. Now, where is that baby bag?" Renee said, looking around.

"You left it in the back office, dear," Leslie told her daughter, and the pair wandered off.

"Thank god." Mary rolled her eyes. "Did you know she's already picked out a place for the wedding?"

"What?" Dalton frowned. "No. That's something Adam and I will do."

"Try telling her that," Mary scoffed and took a sip of wine.

"I won't need to, Adam will."

Mary laughed. "Way to pass the buck."

Dalton grinned and swept his gaze around the room until he found Adam standing with most of Pegasus. Mary linked arms with their father and the pair moved off in search of the buffet.

The party was rocking and rolling. His family had arrived several days ago, and his mom had taken the city by storm. They used the brewery as the location for the engagement party, but that was only after his dad had insisted that the Webers pay for renovations. While it had been mind-boggling to see the number of people showing up to help the Webers get the brewery ready, Dalton was used to his parents shaking things up.

Ace had graciously accepted their help and donations to the unit. After all, they were on a limited government budget since they didn't really exist.

Holden Wreck squeezed around a couple of people and made it to the bar.

"I'll have another beer," Holden told Cooper and then turned to him.

"Hey, boss."

"How are you settling in?" He returned the fist bump from Holden.

"It's taken a fair bit, but Beckett is determined that things at home run smoothly," Holden drawled. The Texas accent thick in the man's deep, growly voice.

"You think he'll return to us full time?"

"If I'm being honest, I'm not sure," Holden said and carefully lifted his beer. "My husband moves to his own beat. See ya."

Dalton chuckled. "See ya."

"You need a refill on that?" Cooper's gravelly voice came from across the bar behind him.

"Yeah, thanks." Dalton handed Cooper his glass. "How are you holding up?"

"I'm okay. I won't say I'm great because that would be a lie, but I'm better than some." Cooper gave a nod to Oliver, who was slowly thumping his way across the room toward where Adam and the rest of the crew stood.

"Yeah, Oliver's itching to get that cast off," Dalton agreed with a chuckle. "So, my mom was researching hearing loss due to an explosion and she found some remarkable things. I'm giving you a heads up, she will approach you and she won't take no for an answer until you've heard her out."

Cooper smirked. "I've already spoken with your mom, and she's introduced herself to my mom…so…yeah."

Dalton laughed and Cooper gave a rueful smile.

"All right, man. Thanks for the refill." He lifted his glass and made a beeline toward Adam.

It was slow going through the crowd and he stopped every so often to answer questions and accept congratulations, but his main focus was on Adam and the happiness in the eyes that continued to hold his.

He could have kicked his youthful self in the ass for letting such a great guy go, but he figured he had to go through what he had in order to understand what he'd lost.

He wouldn't be making that mistake ever again.

Adam

He pulled his gaze from Dalton when his man was caught in conversation again.

Well." Hunter rubbed his hands together. "Does anybody know if Jacob is single?"

Adam whipped his head around, mouth opened in amazement at Hunter, and then darted his eyes to Ace standing across from him. Hunter must have a death wish.

"Touch one hair on Jacob's head and you're a dead man," Ace said, deadly still.

"Whoa… possessive much?" Hunter smirked at their boss and Adam feared for the guy when Ace's big hands clenched. Their boss had let the hair on his face grow and it made the man even more menacing.

When Ace shifted, Hunter tensed, held up his hands, and backed slowly up until he was next to Adam. As if Adam could protect him from a beat down from Ace.

Adam snickered into his glass.

"You do know that Jacob won't take no for an answer about working in the field, don't you?" Eagle told Ace.

"Over my dead body," Ace said on a snarl. It appeared

that Ace had given the idea of Jacob working in the field some thought and had decided against it.

"It will be your dead body if you stand in my way," Jacob snapped from the doorway behind them. It was the one that led to the office's steel door. They'd replaced the exploded wood with metal. To get to Pegasus headquarters, a person would now need to blow through two metal doors.

Adam scooted to the side so Jacob could step up next to him.

Ace looked taken aback.

"Bah, just do like I do, Jacob, and just ignore them and do it anyway," Mason said into his third cup of alcohol.

"If I were you, I'd stay out of this," Gage grumbled.

"Well, then it's a good goddamn thing I'm not you, isn't it?" Mason's nostrils flared.

Gage narrowed his eyes. "You have a smart mouth."

"So I've been told." Mason's chin tipped.

"You're not working in the field," Ace whispered harshly to Jacob. The words traveled beyond their group, bringing Adam's gaze from the standoff between Gage and Mason.

Jacob fisted his hands before he marched across to Ace and glared up into their boss's face.

"I will work in the field and if you try to stop me, I know people who will kick your ass! So, you either train me or I'll fucking go someplace else to do it!"

Ace appeared at a loss for words.

Jacob stood toe to toe with Ace for another moment and then glanced at Hunter. "And yes, I'm single," the young hottie finished.

"Hooah," Eagle said and Hunter snickered.

"Knock it the fuck off," Dalton's growl came from over his shoulder and Adam felt a sigh of relief when his fiancé draped an arm around his shoulders. "This is our engagement party and if you twats screw it up? I will fuck you up," Dalton warned.

Adam laughed. It had been this way since he'd joined Pegasus a month ago. While the team worked like a well-oiled machine during ops, they squabbled and bickered like family during downtime.

The familiar thump of Oliver's cast smacking the brewery's wooden floor reached them. With a cane in one hand, Oliver held the tray of drinks in the other. Adam was just about ready to jump to Oliver's aid when a large man plucked the tray from Oliver's hand and parked it on the bar.

Oliver stopped in his tracks and gazed up into the man's face. Adam thought the stranger looked familiar but wasn't sure.

"Who's that?" he whispered to Dalton, but it was Hunter who spoke.

"That... is my big brother. You might have seen him around here a bit. Police Chief Parker Johnson."

Oliver lifted his cane from the floor and poked the end of the stick into Parker's chest, effectively moving the man out of his way before thumping past and toward them.

Parker shifted around, the man's face a mixture of shock and anger. Maybe the look was shock and something else, because the guy seemed incapable of looking away as Oliver's slim frame moved across the room.

"Hey guys, I was going to bring drinks... but got waylaid by a Neanderthal," Oliver said with a growing smile.

"I'll get it," Jacob said and hurried over to retrieve the tray of drinks. Jacob had to move around Parker, who remained standing and staring for several more seconds before turning abruptly away.

"I don't remember inviting him," Dalton said with a frowning glance at Parker.

"Hush." Adam elbowed Dalton in the side and tossed a glance at Hunter.

"It's all good," Hunter said when Dalton turned an apologetic glance toward him. "He's here on official business."

"Official?" Adam frowned.

"Yeah, he's interviewing one of the new bartenders about an assault charge."

"Since when does a police chief interview people?" Eagle mused.

"Parker has a degree in psychology with a focus on trauma victims," Hunter responded.

"Ah, okay," Eagle said.

"And the interview couldn't wait another day?" Dalton asked with skepticism.

Hunter laughed. "Yeah, well maybe, but our new bartender is skittish and would only meet at the brewery. I haven't actually seen or met the guy, but Parker says it's important that he meet Zack in a place he feels comfortable."

"What's wrong with Zack?" Jacob asked with a frown.

"Like I said, I don't know." Hunter held up his hands.

"Zack is fine," Ace assured Jacob.

"So, you've met the new bartender, Zack?" Adam asked Jacob.

"Yeah, I met him working in a dive bar and offered him a job on the spot," Jacob responded, ignoring the dark frown from Ace.

"This just gets better and better," Adam said with a laugh.

"Hey," Dalton murmured and drew him away from the team before he could probe Jacob with more questions, like when had Jacob gone to a dive bar.

"Yes?" He smiled up into Dalton's face, catching and holding those golden eyes.

"All the drama aside, are you happy?" Dalton laced their fingers.

"Happy? As opposed to this morning when you asked me? Or yesterday and the day before when you asked me the same thing?" He laughed.

Dalton gave him a sheepish grin. "Sorry."

"It's okay, love. I'll keep telling you I'm happy until you believe me. I couldn't be happier if I tried."

Dalton's throat moved with a hard swallow. "Your happiness is the most important thing in the world to me."

And that right there was worth all the pain and suffering he'd endured without Dalton in his life.

Having Dalton say those words to him and so much more over the past month had been a balm to his soul.

"You're it for me, baby. There's no going back now." Adam waggled his eyebrows, drawing a smile from Dalton and eliminating the lines of worry.

"I'm never backing out," Dalton whispered and lowered his head for a kiss.

Adam lifted to his toes and pressed his lips to Dalton's mouth.

A wave of hooting filled the room, then clapping, then beer steins slamming on the bar and other surfaces in succession until, laughing, Adam broke away from the kiss and faced their family and friends.

He lifted his glass to the room.

"Here's to us," Adam shouted and tightened his arm around Dalton's waist.

Dalton's voice rang out loudly and the rest of the people in the room followed suit, lifting their glasses.

"To us!"

The End

Stay tuned for Gage and Mason's story in *Rough* (Operation Justice Force book two), coming soon.

PEGASUS ROSTER

Ace (Cohen Gray)—Commander

Dalton Weber—Second in Command

Adam Campbell

Gage Hillcrest

Mason Taylor

Eagle—Declan Weller

Link—Lincoln Beckett

Jacob Burns

Hunter Johnson

Oliver Rains

Cooper Lancaster

Holden Wreck

Beckett—Samuel Wreck

Maverick Cane

OTHER BOOKS BY REESE

Out for Justice Series
Ricochet
Collide
Rampage
Destruction
Bulletproof
A Phoenix Christmas

Code of Honor Series
Cutting It Close
Risking It All
Bringing It Home
Taking It Slow
Whatever It Takes
Battle It Out
Despite It All
Call It Quits

Operation Justice Force
Lethal—Book 1
Fever (A novella)

Cobalt Security Series
Without Warning
Without Fear

Pacific Northwest Shifter Series
Hunted
Bonded
Marked

ACKNOWLEDGEMENTS

To my fans, as always, these stories are for you.

ABOUT THE AUTHOR

Reese spends her time creating stories from the characters rattling around in her head. Her love of reading mystery, action and adventure, and fantasy books led to her love of writing. Reese works as a full-time writer. She loves to hear from her readers. Check out her website at reeseknightleyauth.wixsite.com/mysite. You can reach her on Facebook, Twitter, TikTok and Instagram. Her email address is Reeseknightleyauthor@gmail.com.

Printed in Great Britain
by Amazon